THE
CHRISTMAS EVE
READER

THE CHRISTMAS EVE READER

A Treasury of Yuletide Stories and Poems for the Whole Family

EDITED BY

JAMES CHARLTON
and BARBARA GILSON

LINE DRAWINGS BY

REISIE NUCERA

DOUBLEDAY & COMPANY, INC.
GARDEN CITY, NEW YORK
1977

Contents

Foreword

Is There A Santa Claus (New York *Sun*)

Twelve Days of Christmas

Christmas at Dingley Dell—*Charles Dickens*

The Little Match-Girl—*Hans Christian Andersen*

Three Kings of Orient—*John Henry Hopkins*

The Gift of the Magi—*O. Henry*

Silent Night, Holy Night—*Joseph Mohr*

Christmas Every Day—*William Dean Howells*

Christmas and New Year Bells—*Alfred Tennyson*

Down Pens—*Saki*

Christmas in a Village—*John Clare*

Christmas with Sir Roger—*Joseph Addison*

The Sheep Herd—*Sister Mariella*

I Take Supper With My Wife
—*Antoine Gustave Droz*

Christmas Carol—*Sara Teasdale*

The Adventure of the Blue Carbuncle
—*Arthur Conan Doyle*

The Three Ships—*Alfred Noyes*

Foreword

"Yes, Virginia, there is a Santa Claus. He exists as certainly as love and generosity and devotion exist, and you know that they abound and give to your life its highest beauty and joy."

That is part of the famous reply to eight-year-old Virginia O'Hanlon, who asked the editor of the New York *Sun* if there was really a Santa Claus. The newspaper has long since disappeared, but the sentiment remains as fresh and true as when it was written eighty years ago. Christmas really is a special time, a time to reflect on and renew those enduring qualities of the holiday season, and a time to remember the peace and joy that is the real essence of Christmas.

Christmas is the most nostalgic of all festive days, and its age old joy is truly reflected in the literature of the holiday. The theme with its many meanings, has been an inspiration for poets, humorists and novelists for centuries.

In keeping with the spirit of the season we offer this Christmas sampler of stories and poems to delight the whole family. Chosen from A CHRISTMAS FEAST published this year by Nelson Doubleday, Inc., this enchanting collection includes a wide range of timeless and meaningful writings. Such favorites as Dickens' *Christmas at Dingley Dell* and Hans Christian Andersen's touching story of the little match-girl are here, as well as O. Henry's *Gift of the Magi*. The witty effervescence of Saki, a little-known adventure of Sherlock Holmes and many others will provide hours of pleasurable reading for everyone, and all enhanced by the delightful line drawings of Reisie Nucera.

If you are coming upon some of these stories for the first time you have a special treat ahead of you. And if you have read some of them before you'll be entranced by the nostalgic journey that is one of the special joys of Christmas.

Jim Charlton & Barbara Gilson
Editors of A CHRISTMAS FEAST

THE
CHRISTMAS EVE
READER

Is There a Santa Claus?

(This famous editorial first appeared in the New York *Sun*, September 21, 1897)

WE TAKE PLEASURE in answering at once and thus prominently the communication below, expressing at the same time our great gratification that its faithful author is numbered among the friends of *The Sun*:

Dear Editor:

I am 8 years old.
Some of my little friends say there is no Santa Claus.
Papa says "If you see it in The Sun it's so."
Please tell me the truth, is there a Santa Claus?

Virginia O'Hanlon
115 West 95th Street

Virginia, your little friends are wrong. They have been affected by the skepticism of a skeptical age. They do not believe except what they see. They think that nothing can be which is not comprehensible by their little minds. All minds, Virginia, whether they be men's or children's, are little. In this great universe of ours man is a mere insect, an ant, in his intellect, as compared with the boundless world about him, as measured by the intelligence capable of grasping the whole of truth and knowledge.

Yes, Virginia, there is a Santa Claus. He exists as certainly as love and generosity and devotion exist, and you know that they abound and give to your life its highest beauty and joy.

Alas! how dreary would be the world if there were no Santa Claus! It would be as dreary as if there were no Virginias. There would be no childlike faith then, no poetry, no romance to make tolerable this existence. We should have no enjoyment, except in sense and sight. The eternal light with which childhood fills the world would be extinguished.

Not believe in Santa Claus! You might as well not believe in fairies! You might get your papa to hire men to watch in all the chimneys on Christmas eve to catch Santa Claus, but even if they did not see Santa Claus coming down, what would that prove? Nobody sees Santa Claus, but that is no sign that there is no Santa Claus. The most real things in the world are those that neither children nor men can see. Did you ever see fairies dancing on the lawn? Of course not, but that's no proof that they are not there. Nobody can conceive or imagine all the wonders there are unseen and unseeable in the world.

You tear apart the baby's rattle and see what makes the noise inside, but there is a veil covering the unseen world which not the strongest man, nor even the united strength of all the strongest men that ever lived, could tear apart. Only faith, fancy, poetry, love, romance, can push aside that curtain and view and picture the supernal beauty and glory beyond. Is it all real? Ah, Virginia, in all this world there is nothing else real and abiding.

No Santa Claus! Thank God he lives, and he lives forever. A thousand years from now, Virginia, nay, ten times ten thousand years from now, he will continue to make glad the heart of childhood.

The Twelve Days of Christmas

(Traditional)

The first day of Christmas
My true love sent to me
A partridge in a pear-tree.

The second day of Christmas
My true love sent to me
Two turtle-doves
And a partridge in a pear-tree.

The third day of Christmas
My true love sent to me
Three French hens,
Two turtle-doves
And a partridge in a pear-tree.

The fourth day of Christmas
My true love sent to me
Four colly birds,
Three French hens,
Two turtle-doves
And a partridge in a pear-tree.

The fifth day of Christmas
My true love sent to me
Five gold rings,
Four colly birds,

Three French hens,
Two turtle-doves
And a partridge in a pear-tree.

The sixth day of Christmas
My true love sent to me
Six geese a-laying,
Five gold rings,
Four colly birds,
Three French hens,
Two turtle-doves
And a partridge in a pear-tree.

The seventh day of Christmas
My true love sent to me
Seven swans a-swimming,
Six geese a-laying,
Five gold rings,
Four colly birds,
Three French hens,
Two turtle-doves
And a partridge in a pear-tree.

The eighth day of Christmas
My true love sent to me
Eight maids a-milking,
Seven swans a-swimming,
Six geese a-laying,
Five gold rings,
Four colly birds,
Three French hens,
Two turtle-doves
And a partridge in a pear-tree.

Twelve Days of Christmas

The ninth day of Christmas
My true love sent to me
Nine drummers drumming,
Eight maids a-milking,
Seven swans a-swimming,
Six geese a-laying,
Five gold rings,
Four colly birds,
Three French hens,
Two turtle-doves
And a partridge in a pear-tree.

The tenth day of Christmas
My true love sent to me
Ten pipers piping,
Nine drummers drumming,
Eight maids a-milking,
Seven swans a-swimming,
Six geese a-laying,
Five gold rings,
Four colly birds,
Three French hens,
Two turtle-doves
And a partridge in a pear-tree.

The eleventh day of Christmas
My true love sent to me
Eleven ladies dancing,
Ten pipers piping,
Nine drummers drumming,
Eight maids a-milking,
Seven swans a-swimming,
Six geese a-laying,
Five gold rings,
Four colly birds,

Three French hens,
Two turtle-doves
And a partridge in a pear-tree.

The twelfth day of Christmas
My true love sent to me
Twelve lords a-leaping,
Eleven ladies dancing,
Ten pipers piping,
Nine drummers drumming,
Eight maids a-milking,
Seven swans a-swimming,
Six geese a-laying,
Five gold rings,
Four colly birds,
Three French hens,
Two turtle-doves
And a partridge in a pear-tree.

Christmas at Dingley Dell

by CHARLES DICKENS

FROM the centre of the ceiling of . . . [the] kitchen, old
Wardle had . . . suspended, with his own hands, a huge
branch of mistletoe, and this same branch of mistletoe instan-
taneously gave rise to a scene of general and delightful struggling and confusion; in the midst of which, Mr. Pickwick,
with a gallantry that would have done honour to a descend-
ant of Lady Tollimglower herself, took the old lady by the
hand, led her beneath the mystic branch, and saluted her in
all courtesy and decorum. The old lady submitted to this
piece of practical politeness with all the dignity which
befitted so important and serious a solemnity, but the
younger ladies, not being so thoroughly imbued with a super-
stitious veneration for the custom; or imagining that the
value of a salute is very much enhanced if it cost a little trouble to obtain it: screamed and struggled, and ran into corners,
and threatened and remonstrated, and did everything but
leave the room, until some of the less adventurous gentlemen
were on the point of desisting, when they all at once found it
useless to resist any longer, and submitted to be kissed with a
good grace . . . Wardle stood with his back to the fire, sur-
veying the whole scene, with the utmost satisfaction; and the
fat boy took the opportunity of appropriating to his own use,
and summarily devouring, a particularly fine mince-pie, that
had been carefully put by for somebody else.

Now, the screaming had subsided, and faces were in a glow,
and curls in a tangle, and Mr. Pickwick, after kissing the old
lady as before mentioned, was standing under the mistletoe,

looking with a very pleased countenance on all that was passing around him, when the young lady with the black eyes, after a little whispering with the other young ladies, made a sudden dart forward, and, putting her arm round Mr. Pickwick's neck, saluted him affectionately on the left cheek; and before Mr. Pickwick distinctly knew what was the matter, he was surrounded by the whole body, and kissed by every one of them.

It was a pleasant thing to see Mr. Pickwick in the centre of the group, now pulled this way, and then that, and first kissed on the chin, and then on the nose, and then on the spectacles: and to hear the peals of laughter which were raised on every side; but it was a still more pleasant thing to see Mr. Pickwick, blinded shortly afterwards with a silk handkerchief, falling up against the wall, and scrambling into corners, and going through all the mysteries of blind-man's buff, with the utmost relish for the game, until at last he caught one of the poor relations, and then had to evade the blindman himself, which he did with a nimbleness and agility that elicited the admiration and applause of all beholders. The poor relations caught the people who they thought would like it, and, when the game flagged, got caught themselves. When they were all tired of blind-man's buff, there was a great game at snapdragon, and when fingers enough were burned with that, and all the raisins were gone, they sat down by the huge fire of blazing logs to a substantial supper, and a mighty bowl of wassail, something smaller than an ordinary wash-house copper, in which the hot apples were hissing and bubbling with a rich look, and a jolly sound, that were perfectly irresistible.

"This," said Mr. Pickwick, looking around him, "this is, indeed, comfort."

"Our invariable custom," replied Mr. Wardle. "Everybody sits down with us on Christmas eve, as you see them now—servants and all; and here we wait, until the clock strikes twelve, to usher Christmas in, and beguile the time with forfeits and old stories. Trundle, my boy, rake up the fire."

Up flew the bright sparks in myriads as the logs were stirred. The deep red blaze sent forth a rich glow, that penetrated into the furthest corner of the room, and cast its cheerful tint on every face . . .

"How it snows!" said one of the men, in a low tone.

"Snows, does it?" said Wardle.

"Rough, cold night, sir," replied the man; "and there's a wind got up, that drifts it across the fields, in a thick white cloud."

"What does Jem say?" inquired the old lady. "There ain't anything the matter, is there?"

"No, no, mother," replied Wardle; "he says there's a snowdrift, and a wind that's piercing cold. I should know that, by the way it rumbles in the chimney."

"Ah!" said the old lady, "there was just such a wind, and just such a fall of snow, a good many years back, I recollect—just five years before your poor father died. It was a Christmas eve, too; and I remember that on that very night he told us the story about the goblins that carried away old Gabriel Grub."

"The story about what?" said Mr. Pickwick.

"Oh, nothing, nothing," replied Wardle. "About an old sexton, that the good people down here suppose to have been carried away by goblins."

"Suppose!" ejaculated the old lady. "Is there anybody hardy enough to disbelieve it? Suppose! Haven't you heard ever since you were a child, that he *was* carried away by the goblins, and don't you know he was?"

"Very well, mother, he was, if you like," said Wardle, laughing. "He *was* carried away by goblins, Pickwick; and there's an end of the matter."

"No, no," said Mr. Pickwick, "not an end of it, I assure you; for I must hear how, and why, and all about it."

Wardle smiled, as every head was bent forward to hear; and filling out the wassail with no stinted hand, nodded a health to Mr. Pickwick, and began as follows:

The Story of the Goblins Who Stole a Sexton

"IN an old abbey town, down in this part of the country, a long, long while ago—so long, that the story must be a true one, because our great grandfathers implicitly believed it—there officiated as sexton and grave-digger in the churchyard, one Gabriel Grub. It by no means follows that because a man is a sexton, and constantly surrounded by the emblems of mortality, therefore he should be a morose and melancholy man; your undertakers are the merriest fellows in the world; and I once had the honour of being on intimate terms with a mute, who in private life, and off duty, was as comical and jocose a little fellow as ever chirped out a devil-may-care song, without a hitch in his memory, or drained off the contents of a good stiff glass without stopping for breath. But, notwithstanding these precedents to the contrary, Gabriel Grub was an ill-conditioned, cross-grained, surly fellow—a morose and lonely man, who consorted with nobody but himself, and an old wicker bottle which fitted into his large deep waistcoat pocket—and who eyed each merry face, as it passed him by, with such a deep scowl of malice and ill-humour, as it was difficult to meet, without feeling something the worse for.

"A little before twilight, one Christmas eve, Gabriel shouldered his spade, lighted his lantern, and betook himself towards the old churchyard; for he had got a grave to finish by next morning, and, feeling very low, he thought it might raise his spirits, perhaps, if he went on with his work at once. As he went his way, up the ancient street, he saw the cheerful light of the blazing fires gleam through the old casements, and heard the loud laugh and the cheerful shouts of those who

were assembled around them; he marked the bustling prepa-
rations for next day's cheer, and smelt the numerous savoury
odours consequent thereupon, as they steamed up from the
kitchen windows in clouds. All this was gall and wormwood
to the heart of Gabriel Grub; and when groups of children
bounded out of the houses, tripped across the road, and were
met, before they could knock at the opposite door, by half a
dozen curly-headed little rascals who crowded round them as
they flocked up-stairs to spend the evening in their Christmas
games, Gabriel smiled grimly, and clutched the handle of his
spade with a firmer grasp, as he thought of measles, scarlet-
fever, thrush, whooping-cough, and a good many other
sources of consolation besides.

"In this happy frame of mind, Gabriel strode along: returning a short, sullen growl to the good-humoured greetings
of such of his neighbours as now and then passed him: until
he turned into the dark lane which led to the churchyard.
Now, Gabriel had been looking forward to reaching the dark
lane, because it was, generally speaking, a nice, gloomy,
mournful place, into which the towns-people did not much
care to go, except in broad daylight, and when the sun was
shining; consequently, he was not a little indignant to hear a
young urchin roaring out some jolly song about a merry
Christmas, in this very sanctuary, which had been called
Coffin Lane ever since the days of the old abbey, and the time
of the shaven-headed monks. As Gabriel walked on, and the
voice drew nearer, he found it proceeded from a small boy,
who was hurrying along, to join one of the little parties in the
old street, and who, partly to keep himself company, and
partly to prepare himself for the occasion, was shouting out
the song at the highest pitch of his lungs. So Gabriel waited
until the boy came up, and then dodged him into a corner,
and rapped him over the head with his lantern five or six
times, to teach him to modulate his voice. And as the boy
hurried away with his hand to his head, singing quite a

different sort of tune, Gabriel Grub chuckled very heartily to himself, and entered the churchyard: locking the gate behind him.

"He took off his coat, put down his lantern, and getting into the unfinished grave, worked at it for an hour or so, with right good will. But the earth was hardened with the frost, and it was no very easy matter to break it up, and shovel it out; and although there was a moon, it was a very young one, and shed little light upon the grave, which was in the shadow of the church. At any other time, these obstacles would have made Gabriel Grub very moody and miserable, but he was so well pleased with having stopped the small boy's singing, that he took little heed of the scanty progress he had made, and looked down into the grave, when he had finished work for the night, with grim satisfaction: murmuring as he gathered up his things:

> *Brave lodgings for one, brave lodgings for one,*
> *A few feet of cold earth, when life is done;*
> *A stone at the head, a stone at the feet,*
> *A rich, juicy meal for the worms to eat;*
> *Rank grass overhead, and damp clay around,*
> *Brave lodgings for one, these, in holy ground!*

"'Ho! ho!' laughed Gabriel Grub, as he sat himself down on a flat tombstone which was a favourite resting-place of his; and drew forth his wicker bottle. 'A coffin at Christmas! A Christmas Box. Ho! ho! ho!'

"'Ho! ho! ho!' repeated a voice which sounded close behind him.

"Gabriel paused in some alarm, in the act of raising the wicker bottle to his lips; and looked round. The bottom of the oldest grave about him, was not more still and quiet, than the churchyard in the pale moonlight. The cold hoarfrost glistened on the tombstones, and sparkled like rows of gems, among the stone carvings of the old church. The snow lay hard and crisp upon the ground; and spread over the thickly strewn mounds of earth so white and smooth a cover that it seemed as if corpses lay there, hidden only by their winding sheets. Not the faintest rustle broke the profound tranquillity of the solemn scene. Sound itself appeared to be frozen up, all was so cold and still.

" 'It was the echoes,' said Gabriel Grub, raising the bottle to his lips again.

" 'It was *not*,' said a deep voice.

"Gabriel started up, and stood rooted to the spot with astonishment and terror; for his eyes rested on a form that made his blood run cold.

"Seated on an upright tombstone, close to him, was a strange unearthly figure, whom Gabriel felt at once, was no being of this world. His long fantastic legs which might have reached the ground, were cocked up, and crossed after a quaint, fantastic fashion; his sinewy arms were bare; and his hands rested on his knees. On his short round body, he wore a close covering, ornamented with small slashes; a short cloak dangled at his back; the collar was cut into curious peaks, which served the goblin in lieu of ruff or neckerchief; and his shoes curled up at his toes into long points. On his head, he wore a broad-brimmed sugar-loaf hat, garnished with a single feather. The hat was covered with the white frost; and the goblin looked as if he had sat on the same tombstone very comfortably, for two or three hundred years. He was sitting perfectly still; his tongue was put out, as if in derision; and he was grinning at Gabriel Grub with such a grin as only a goblin could call up.

" 'It was *not* the echoes,' said the goblin.

"Gabriel Grub was paralysed, and could make no reply.

" 'What do you do here on Christmas eve?' said the goblin sternly.

" 'I came to dig a grave, sir,' stammered Gabriel Grub.

" 'What man wanders among graves and churchyards on such a night as this?' cried the goblin.

" 'Gabriel Grub! Gabriel Grub!' screamed a wild chorus of voices that seemed to fill the churchyard. Gabriel looked fearfully round—nothing was to be seen.

" 'What have you got in that bottle?' said the goblin.

" 'Hollands, sir,' replied the sexton, trembling more than ever; for he had bought it of the smugglers, and he thought that perhaps his questioner might be in the excise department of the goblins.

" 'Who drinks Hollands alone, and in a churchyard, on such a night as this?' said the goblin.

" 'Gabriel Grub! Gabriel Grub!' exclaimed the wild voices again.

"The goblin leered maliciously at the terrified sexton, and then raising his voice, exclaimed:

" 'And who, then, is our fair and lawful prize?'

"To this inquiry the invisible chorus replied, in a strain that sounded like the voices of many choristers singing to the mighty swell of the old church organ—a strain that seemed borne to the sexton's ears upon a wild wind, and to die away as it passed onward; but the burden of the reply was still the same, 'Gabriel Grub! Gabriel Grub!'

"The goblin grinned a broader grin than before, as he said, 'Well, Gabriel, what do you say to this?'

"The sexton gasped for breath.

" 'What do you think of this, Gabriel?' said the goblin, kicking up his feet in the air on either side of the tombstone, and looking at the turned-up points with as much complacency as if he had been contemplating the most fashionable pair of Wellingtons in all Bond Street.

" 'It's—it's—very curious, sir,' replied the sexton, half dead with fright; 'very curious, and very pretty, but I think I'll go back and finish my work, sir, if you please.'

" 'Work!' said the goblin, 'what work?'

" 'The grave, sir; making the grave,' stammered the sexton.

" 'Oh, the grave, eh?' said the goblin; 'who makes graves at a time when all other men are merry, and takes a pleasure in it?'

"Again the mysterious voices replied, 'Gabriel Grub! Gabriel Grub!'

" 'I'm afraid my friends want you, Gabriel,' said the goblin, thrusting his tongue further into his cheek than ever—and a most astonishing tongue it was—'I'm afraid my friends want you, Gabriel,' said the goblin.

" 'Under favour, sir,' replied the horror-stricken sexton, 'I don't think they can, sir; they don't know me, sir; I don't think the gentlemen have ever seen me, sir.'

" 'Oh yes, they have,' replied the goblin; 'we know the man with the sulky face and grim scowl, that came down the street to-night, throwing his evil looks at the children, and grasping his burying spade the tighter. We know the man who struck the boy in the envious malice of his heart, because the boy could be merry, and he could not. We know him, we know him.'

"Here, the goblin gave a loud shrill laugh, which the echoes returned twenty-fold: and throwing his legs up in the air, stood upon his head, or rather upon the very point of his sugar-loaf hat, on the narrow edge of the tombstone: whence he threw a somerset with extraordinary agility, right to the sexton's feet, at which he planted himself in the attitude in which tailors generally sit upon the shopboard.

" 'I—I—am afraid I must leave you, sir,' said the sexton, making an effort to move.

" 'Leave us!' said the goblin, 'Gabriel Grub going to leave us. Ho! ho! ho!'

"As the goblin laughed, the sexton observed, for one instant, a brilliant illumination within the windows of the church, as if the whole building were lighted up; it disappeared, the organ pealed forth a lively air, and whole troops of goblins, the very counterpart of the first one, poured into the churchyard, and began playing at leap-frog with the tomb-stones: never stopping for an instant to take breath, but 'over-ing' the highest among them, one after the other, with the most marvellous dexterity. The first goblin was a most as-tonishing leaper, and none of the others could come near him; even in the extremity of his terror the sexton could not help observing, that while his friends were content to leap over the common-sized gravestones, the first one took the family vaults, iron railings and all, with as much ease as if they had been so many street posts. At last the game reached to a most exciting pitch; the organ played quicker and quicker; and the goblins leaped faster and faster: coiling themselves up, rolling head over heels upon the ground, and bounding over the tombstones like foot-balls. The sexton's brain whirled round with the rapidity of the motion he be-held, and his legs reeled beneath him, as the spirits flew be-fore his eyes: when the goblin king, suddenly darting towards him, laid his hand upon his collar, and sank with him through the earth.

"When Gabriel Grub had had time to fetch his breath, which the rapidity of his descent had for the moment taken away, he found himself in what appeared to be a large cavern, surrounded on all sides by crowds of goblins, ugly and grim; in the centre of the room, on an elevated seat, was stationed his friend of the churchyard; and close beside him stood Gabriel Grub himself, without power of motion.

"'Cold to-night,' said the king of goblins, 'very cold. A glass of something warm, here!'

"At this command, half a dozen officious goblins, with a perpetual smile upon their faces, whom Gabriel Grub imag-ined to be courtiers, on that account, hastily disappeared, and presently returned with a goblet of liquid fire, which they presented to the king.

"'Ah!' cried the goblin, whose cheeks and throat were

transparent, as he tossed down the flame, 'this warms one, indeed! Bring a bumper of the same for Mr. Grub.'

"It was in vain for the unfortunate sexton to protest that he was not in the habit of taking anything warm at night; one of the goblins held him while another poured the blazing liquid down his throat; the whole assembly screeched with laughter as he coughed and choked, and wiped away the tears which gushed plentifully from his eyes, after swallowing the burning draught.

"'And now,' said the king, fantastically poking the taper corner of his sugar-loaf hat into the sexton's eyes, and thereby occasioning him the most exquisite pain: 'And now, show the man of misery and gloom, a few of the pictures from our own great storehouse!'

"As the goblin said this, a thick cloud which obscured the remoter end of the cavern, rolled gradually away, and disclosed, apparently at a great distance, a small and scantily furnished, but neat and clean apartment. A crowd of little children were gathered round a bright fire, clinging to their mother's gown, and gambolling around her chair. The mother occasionally rose, and drew aside the window-curtain, as if to look for some expected object; a frugal meal was ready spread upon the table, and an elbow chair was placed near the fire. A knock was heard at the door; the mother opened it, and the children crowded round her, and clapped their hands for joy, as their father entered. He was wet and weary, and shook the snow from his garments, as the children crowded round him, and seizing his cloak, hat, stick, and gloves, with busy zeal, ran with them from the room. Then, as he sat down to his meal before the fire, the children climbed about his knee, and the mother sat by his side, and all seemed happiness and comfort.

"But a change came upon the view, almost imperceptibly. The scene was altered to a small bed-room, where the fairest and youngest child lay dying; the roses had fled from his cheek, and the light from the eye; and even as the sexton looked upon him with an interest he had never felt or known before, he died. His young brothers and sisters crowded round his little bed, and seized his tiny hand, so cold and heavy; but they shrunk back from its touch, and looked with awe on his infant face; for calm and tranquil as it was and sleeping in rest and peace as the beautiful child seemed to be, they saw that he was dead, and they knew that he was an Angel looking down upon, and blessing them, from a bright and happy Heaven.

"Again the light cloud passed across the picture, and again the subject changed. The father and mother were old and helpless now, and the number of those about them was diminished more than half; but content and cheerfulness sat on every face, and beamed in every eye, as they crowded round the fireside, and told and listened to old stories of earlier and bygone days. Slowly and peacefully, the father sank into the grave, and, soon after, the sharer of all his cares and troubles followed him to a place of rest. The few, who yet survived them, knelt by their tomb, and watered the green turf which covered it, with their tears; then rose, and turned away: sadly and mournfully, but not with bitter cries, or despairing lamentations, for they knew that they should one day meet again; and once more they mixed with the busy world, and their content and cheerfulness were restored. The cloud settled upon the picture, and concealed it from the sexton's view.

"'What do you think of *that?*' said the goblin, turning his large face towards Gabriel Grub.

"Gabriel murmured out something about its being very pretty, and looked somewhat ashamed, as the goblin bent his fiery eyes upon him.

"'*You* a miserable man!' said the goblin, in a tone of excessive contempt. 'You!' He appeared disposed to add more, but indignation choked his utterance, so he lifted up one of his very pliable legs, and flourishing it above his head a little, to insure his aim, administered a good sound kick to Gabriel Grub; immediately after which, all the goblins in waiting crowded round the wretched sexton, and kicked him without mercy: according to the established and invariable custom of courtiers upon earth, who kick whom royalty kicks, and hug whom royalty hugs.

" 'Show him some more!' said the king of the goblins.

"At these words, the cloud was dispelled, and a rich and beautiful landscape was disclosed to view—there is just such another, to this day, within half a mile of the old abbey town. The sun shone from out the clear blue sky, the water sparkled beneath its rays, and the trees looked greener, and the flowers more gay, beneath his cheering influence. The water rippled on, with a pleasant sound; the trees rustled in the light wind that murmured among their leaves; the birds sang upon the boughs; and the lark carolled on high her welcome to the morning. Yes, it was morning; the bright, balmy morning of summer; the minutest leaf, the smallest blade of grass, was instinct with life. The ant crept forth to her daily toil, the butterfly fluttered and basked in the warm rays of the sun; myriads of insects spread their transparent wings, and revelled in their brief but happy existence. Man walked forth, elated with the scene; and all was brightness and splendour.

" 'You a miserable man!' said the king of the goblins, in a more contemptuous tone than before. And again the king of the goblins gave his leg a flourish; again it descended on the shoulders of the sexton; and again the attendant goblins imitated the example of their chief.

"Many a time the cloud went and came, and many a lesson it taught to Gabriel Grub, who, although his shoulders smarted with pain from the frequent applications of the goblins' feet, looked on with an interest that nothing could diminish. He saw that men who worked hard, and earned their scanty bread with lives of labour, were cheerful and happy; and that to the most ignorant, the sweet face of nature was a never-failing source of cheerfulness and joy. He saw those who had been delicately nurtured, and tenderly brought up, cheerful under privations, and superior to suffering that would have crushed many of a rougher grain, because they bore within their own bosoms the materials of happiness, contentment, and peace. He saw that women, the tenderest and most fragile of all God's creatures, were the oftenest superior to sorrow, adversity, and distress; and he saw that it was because they bore, in their own hearts, an inexhaustible wellspring of affection and devotion. Above all, he saw that men like himself, who snarled at the mirth and cheerfulness of others, were the foulest weeds on the fair surface of the earth; and setting all the good of the world against the evil, he came to the conclusion that it was a very decent and respectable sort of world after all. No sooner had he formed it, than the cloud which closed over the last picture, seemed to settle on his senses, and lull him to repose. One by one, the goblins faded from his sight; and as the last one disappeared, he sunk to sleep.

"The day had broken when Gabriel Grub awoke, and found himself lying, at full length on the flat gravestone in the churchyard, with the wicker bottle lying empty by his side, and his coat, spade, and lantern, all well whitened by the last night's frost, scattered on the ground. The stone on which he had first seen the goblin seated stood bolt upright before him, and the grave at which he had worked, the night before, was not far off. At first, he began to doubt the reality of his adventures, but the acute pain in his shoulders when he attempted to rise assured him that the kicking of the goblins was certainly not ideal. He was staggered again by observing no traces of footsteps in the snow on which the goblins had played at leap-frog with the gravestones, but he speedily accounted for this circumstance when he remembered that, being spirits, they would leave no visible impression behind them. So, Gabriel Grub got on his feet as well as he could, for the pain in his back; and brushing the frost off his coat, put it on, and turned his face towards the town.

"But he was an altered man, and he could not bear the thought of returning to a place where his repentance would be scoffed at, and his reformation disbelieved. He hesitated for a few moments; and then turned away to wander where he might, and seek his bread elsewhere.

"The lantern, the spade, and the wicker bottle, were found, that day, in the churchyard. There were a great many speculations about the sexton's fate, at first, but it was speedily determined that he had been carried away by the goblins; and there were not wanting some very credible witnesses who had distinctly seen him whisked through the air on the back of a chestnut horse blind of one eye, with the hind-quarters of a lion, and the tail of a bear. At length all this was devoutly believed; and the new sexton used to exhibit to the curious, for a trifling emolument, a good-sized piece of the church weathercock which had been accidentally kicked off by the aforesaid horse in his aerial flight, and picked up by himself in the churchyard, a year or two afterwards.

"Unfortunately, these stories were somewhat disturbed by the unlooked-for re-appearance of Gabriel Grub himself, some ten years afterwards, a ragged, contented, rheumatic old man. He told his story to the clergyman, and also to the mayor; and in course of time it began to be received, as a matter of history, in which form it has continued down to this very day. The believers in the weathercock tale, having misplaced their confidence once, were not easily prevailed upon to part with it again, so they looked as wise as they could, shrugged their shoulders, touched their foreheads, and murmured something about Gabriel Grub having drunk all the Hollands, and then fallen asleep on the flat tombstone; and they affected to explain what he supposed he had witnessed in the goblin's cavern, by saying that he had seen the world, and grown wiser. But this opinion, which was by no means a

popular one at any time, gradually died off; and be the matter
how it may, as Gabriel Grub was afflicted with rheumatism to
the end of his days, this story has at least one moral, if it
teach no better one—and that is, that if a man turn sulky and
drink by himself at Christmas time, he may make up his
mind to be not a bit the better for it: let the spirits be never
so good, or let them be even as many degrees beyond proof, as
those which Gabriel Grub saw in the goblin's cavern."

*   *   *

"Well, Sam," said Mr. Pickwick as that favoured servitor
entered his bed-chamber with his warm water, on the morning of Christmas day, "still frosty?"

"Water in the wash-hand basin's a mask o' ice, sir," re-
sponded Sam.

"Severe weather, Sam," observed Mr. Pickwick.

"Fine time for them as is well wropped up, as the Polar
Bear said to himself, ven he was practising his skating," replied Mr. Weller.

"I shall be down in a quarter of an hour, Sam," said Mr.
Pickwick, untying his nightcap.

"Wery good, sir," replied Sam . . .

"Now," said Wardle, after a substantial lunch, with the
agreeable items of strong beer and cherry-brandy, had been
done ample justice to; "what say you to an hour on the ice?
We shall have plenty of time."

"Capital!" said Mr. Benjamin Allen.

"Prime!" ejaculated Mr. Bob Sawyer.

"You skate, of course, Winkle?" said Wardle.

"Ye-es; oh, yes," replied Mr. Winkle. "I—I—am *rather* out
of practice."

"Oh, *do* skate, Mr. Winkle," said Arabella. "I like to see it
so much."

"Oh, it is *so* graceful," said another young lady.

A third young lady said it was elegant, and a fourth expressed her opinion that it was "swan-like."

"I should be very happy, I'm sure," said Mr. Winkle, reddening; "but I have no skates."

This objection was at once overruled. Trundle had a couple of pair, and the fat boy announced that there were half-a-dozen more down-stairs: whereat Mr. Winkle expressed exquisite delight, and looked exquisitely uncomfortable.

Old Wardle led the way to a pretty large sheet of ice; and the fat boy and Mr. Weller, having shovelled and swept away the snow which had fallen on it during the night, Mr. Bob Sawyer adjusted his skates with a dexterity which to Mr. Winkle was perfectly marvellous and described circles with his left leg, and cut figures of eight, and inscribed upon the ice, without once stopping for breath, a great many other pleasant and astonishing devices, to the excessive satisfaction of Mr. Pickwick, Mr. Tupman, and the ladies: which reached a pitch of positive enthusiasm, when old Wardle and Benjamin Allen, assisted by the aforesaid Bob Sawyer, performed some mystic evolutions, which they called a reel.

All this time, Mr. Winkle, with his face and hands blue with the cold, had been forcing a gimlet into the soles of his feet, and putting his skates on, with the points behind, and getting the straps into a very complicated and entangled state, with the assistance of Mr. Snodgrass, who knew rather less about skates than a Hindoo. At length, however, with the assistance of Mr. Weller, the unfortunate skates were firmly screwed and buckled on, and Mr. Winkle was raised to his feet.

"Now, then, sir," said Sam, in an encouraging tone; "off vith you, and show 'em how to do it."

"Stop, Sam, stop!" said Mr. Winkle, trembling violently, and clutching hold of Sam's arms with the grasp of a drowning man. "How slippery it is, Sam!"

"Not an uncommon thing upon ice, sir," replied Mr. Weller. "Hold up, sir!"

This last observation of Mr. Weller's bore reference to a demonstration Mr. Winkle made at the instant, of a frantic desire to throw his feet in the air, and dash the back of his head on the ice.

"These—these—are very awkward skates; ain't they, Sam?" inquired Mr. Winkle, staggering.

"I'm afeerd there's a orkard gen'l'm'n in 'em, sir," replied Sam.

"Now, Winkle," cried Mr. Pickwick, quite unconscious that there was anything the matter. "Come; the ladies are all anxiety."

"Yes, yes," replied Mr. Winkle, with a ghastly smile. "I'm coming."

"Just a goin' to begin," said Sam, endeavouring to disengage himself. "Now, sir, start off!"

"Stop an instant, Sam," gasped Mr. Winkle, clinging most affectionately to Mr. Weller. "I find I've got a couple of coats at home that I don't want, Sam. You may have them, Sam."

"Thank'ee, sir," replied Mr. Weller.

"Never mind touching your hat, Sam," said Mr. Winkle, hastily. "You needn't take your hand away to do that. I meant to have given you five shillings this morning for a Christmas-box, Sam. I'll give it you this afternoon, Sam."

"You're wery good, sir," replied Mr. Weller.

"Just hold me at first, Sam; will you?" said Mr. Winkle. "There—that's right. I shall soon get in the way of it, Sam. Not too fast, Sam; not too fast."

Mr. Winkle stooping forward, with his body half doubled up, was being assisted over the ice by Mr. Weller, in a very singular and un-swan-like manner, when Mr. Pickwick most innocently shouted from the opposite bank:

"Sam!"

"Sir?"

"Here. I want you."

"Let go, sir," said Sam. "Don't you hear the governor a callin'? Let go, sir."

With a violent effort, Mr. Weller disengaged himself from the grasp of the agonised Pickwickian, and, in so doing, administered a considerable impetus to the unhappy Mr. Winkle. With an accuracy which no degree of dexterity or practice could have insured, that unfortunate gentleman bore swiftly down into the centre of the reel, at the very moment when Mr. Bob Sawyer was performing a flourish of unparalleled beauty. Mr. Winkle struck wildly against him, and with a loud crash they both fell heavily down. Mr. Pickwick ran to the spot. Bob Sawyer had risen to his feet, but Mr. Winkle was far too wise to do anything of the kind, in skates. He was seated on the ice, making spasmodic efforts to smile; but anguish was depicted on every lineament of his countenance. . . .

"Lift him up," said Mr. Pickwick. Sam assisted him to rise.

Mr. Pickwick retired a few paces apart from the bystanders; and, beckoning his friend to approach, fixed a searching look upon him, and uttered in a low, but distinct and emphatic tone, these remarkable words: "You're a humbug, sir."

"A what?" said Mr. Winkle, starting.

"A humbug, sir. I will speak plainer, if you wish it. An impostor, sir."

With those words, Mr. Pickwick turned slowly on his heel, and rejoined his friends.

While Mr. Pickwick was delivering himself of the sentiment just recorded, Mr. Weller and the fat boy, having by their joint endeavours cut out a slide, were exercising themselves thereupon, in a very masterly and brilliant manner. Sam Weller, in particular, was displaying that beautiful feat of fancy-sliding which is currently denominated "knocking at the cobbler's door," and which is achieved by skimming over the ice on one foot, and occasionally giving a postman's knock upon it with the other. It was a good long slide, and there was something in the motion which Mr. Pickwick, who was very cold with standing still, could not help envying.

"It looks a nice warm exercise that, doesn't it?" he inquired of Wardle, when that gentleman was thoroughly out of breath, by reason of the indefatigable manner in which he had converted his legs into a pair of compasses, and drawn complicated problems on the ice.

"Ah, it does indeed," replied Wardle. "Do you slide?"

"I used to do so, on the gutters, when I was a boy," replied Mr. Pickwick.

"Try it now," said Wardle.

"Oh, do, please, Mr. Pickwick!" cried all the ladies.

"I should be very happy to afford you any amusement," replied Mr. Pickwick, "but I haven't done such a thing these thirty years."

"Pooh! Pooh! Nonsense!" said Wardle, dragging off his skates with the impetuosity which characterised all his proceedings. "Here; I'll keep you company; come along!" And away went the good-tempered old fellow down the slide, with a rapidity which came very close upon Mr. Weller, and beat the fat boy all to nothing.

Mr. Pickwick paused, considered, pulled off his gloves and put them in his hat: took two or three short runs, baulked himself as often, and at last took another run, and went slowly and gravely down the slide, with his feet about a yard and a quarter apart, amidst the gratified shouts of all the spectators.

"Keep the pot a bilin', sir!" said Sam; and down went Wardle again, and then Mr. Pickwick, and then Sam, and then Mr. Winkle, and then Mr. Bob Sawyer, and then the fat boy, and then Mr. Snodgrass, following closely upon each other's heels, and running after each other with as much eagerness as if all their future prospects in life depended on their expedition.

It was the most intensely interesting thing, to observe the manner in which Mr. Pickwick performed his share in the ceremony; to watch the torture of anxiety with which he viewed the person behind, gaining upon him at the imminent hazard of tripping him up; to see him gradually expend the painful force he had put on at first, and turn slowly round on the slide, with his face towards the point from which he had started; to contemplate the playful smile which mantled on his face when he had accomplished the distance, and the eagerness with which he turned round when he had done so, and ran after his predecessor: his black gaiters tripping pleasantly through the snow, and his eyes beaming cheerfulness and gladness through his spectacles. And when he was knocked down (which happened upon the average every third round), it was the most invigorating sight that can possibly be imagined, to behold him gather up his hat, gloves, and handkerchief, with a glowing countenance, and resume his station in the rank, with an ardour and enthusiasm that nothing could abate.

The sport was at its height, the sliding was at the quickest, the laughter was at the loudest, when a sharp smart crack was heard. There was a quick rush towards the bank, a wild scream from the ladies, and a shout from Mr. Tupman. A large mass of ice disappeared; the water bubbled up over it; Mr. Pickwick's hat, gloves, and handkerchief were floating on the surface; and this was all of Mr. Pickwick that anybody could see.

Dismay and anguish were depicted on every countenance, the males turned pale, and the females fainted. Mr. Snodgrass and Mr. Winkle grasped each other by the hand and gazed at the spot where their leader had gone down, with frenzied eagerness: while Mr. Tupman, by way of rendering the promptest assistance, and at the same time conveying to any persons who might be within hearing, the clearest possible notion of the catastrophe, ran off across the country at his utmost speed, screaming "Fire!" with all his might.

It was at this moment, when old Wardle and Sam Weller were approaching the hole with cautious steps, and Mr. Benjamin Allen was holding a hurried consultation with Mr. Bob Sawyer, on the advisability of bleeding the company generally, as an improving little bit of professional practice—it was at this very moment, that a face, head, and shoulders, emerged from beneath the water, and disclosed the features and spectacles of Mr. Pickwick.

"Keep yourself up for an instant—for only one instant!" bawled Mr. Snodgrass.

"Yes, do; let me implore you—for my sake!" roared Mr. Winkle, deeply affected. The adjuration was rather unnecessary; the probability being, that if Mr. Pickwick had declined to keep himself up for anybody else's sake, it would have occurred to him that he might as well do so, for his own.

"Do you feel the bottom there, old fellow?" said Wardle.

"Yes, certainly," replied Mr. Pickwick, wringing the water from his head and face, and gasping for breath. "I fell upon my back. I couldn't get on my feet at first."

The clay upon so much of Mr. Pickwick's coat as was yet visible, bore testimony to the accuracy of this statement; and as the fears of the spectators were still further relieved by the fat boy's suddenly recollecting that the water was nowhere more than five feet deep, prodigies of valour were performed to get him out. After a vast quantity of splashing, and cracking, and struggling, Mr. Pickwick was at length fairly extricated from his unpleasant position, and once more stood on dry land.

"Oh, he'll catch his death of cold," said Emily.

"Dear old thing!" said Arabella. "Let me wrap this shawl round you, Mr. Pickwick."

"Ah, that's the best thing you can do," said Wardle, "and

when you've got it on, run home as fast as your legs can carry you, and jump into bed directly."

A dozen shawls were offered on the instant. Three or four of the thickest having been selected, Mr. Pickwick was wrapped up, and started off, under the guidance of Mr. Weller: presenting the singular phenomenon of an elderly gentleman, dripping wet, and without a hat, with his arms bound down to his sides, skimming over the ground, without any clearly defined purpose, at the rate of six good English miles an hour.

But Mr. Pickwick cared not for appearances in such an extreme case, and urged on by Sam Weller, he kept at the very top of his speed until he reached the door of Manor Farm, where Mr. Tupman had arrived some five minutes before, and had frightened the old lady into palpitations of the heart by impressing her with the unalterable conviction that the kitchen chimney was on fire—a calamity which always presented itself in glowing colours to the old lady's mind, when anybody about her evinced the smallest agitation.

Mr. Pickwick paused not an instant until he was snug in bed. Sam Weller lighted a blazing fire in the room, and took up his dinner; a bowl of punch was carried up afterwards, and a grand carouse held in honour of his safety. Old Wardle would not hear of his rising, so they made the bed the chair, and Mr. Pickwick presided. A second and a third bowl were ordered in; and when Mr. Pickwick awoke next morning, there was not a symptom of rheumatism about him: which proves, as Mr. Bob Sawyer very justly observed, that there is nothing like hot punch in such cases: and that if ever hot punch did fail to act as a preventive, it was merely because the patient fell into the vulgar error of not taking enough of it.

The Little Match-Girl

by HANS CHRISTIAN ANDERSEN

IT WAS terribly cold; it snowed and was already almost dark, and evening came on, the last evening of the year. In the cold and gloom a poor little girl, bareheaded and barefoot, was walking through the streets. When she left her own house she certainly had had slippers on, but of what use were they? They were very big slippers, and her mother had used them till then, so big were they. The little maid lost them as she slipped across the road, where two carriages were rattling by terribly fast. One slipper was not to be found again, and a boy had seized the other and run away with it. He thought he could use it very well as a cradle some day when he had children of his own. So now the little girl went with her little naked feet, which were quite red and blue with the cold. In an old apron she carried a number of matches, and a bundle of them in her hand. No one had bought anything of her all day, and no one had given her a farthing.

Shivering with cold and hunger, she crept along, a picture of misery, poor little girl! The snowflakes covered her long fair hair, which fell in pretty curls over her neck; but she did not think of that now. In all the windows lights were shining, and there was a glorious smell of roast goose, for it was New Year's Eve. Yes, she thought of that!

In a corner formed by two houses, one of which projected beyond the other, she sat down, cowering. She had drawn up her little feet, but she was still colder, and she did not dare to go home, for she had sold no matches and did not bring a farthing of money. From her father she would certainly receive a beating; and, besides, it was cold at home, for they had nothing over them but a roof through which the wind whistled, though the largest rents had been stopped with straw and rags.

Her little hands were almost benumbed with the cold. Ah, a match might do her good, if she could only draw one from the bundle and rub it against the wall and warm her hands at it. She drew one out. R-r-atch! how it sputtered and burned! It was a warm, bright flame, like a little candle, when she held her hands over it; it was a wonderful little light! It really seemed to the little girl as if she sat before a great polished stove with bright brass feet and a brass cover. How the fire burned! How comfortable it was! But the little flame went out, the stove vanished, and she had only the remains of the burnt match in her hand.

A second was rubbed against the wall. It burned up, and when the light fell upon the wall it became transparent like a thin veil, and she could see through it into the room. On the table a snow-white cloth was spread; upon it stood a shining dinner service; the roast goose smoked gloriously, stuffed with apples and dried plums. And, what was still more splendid to behold, the goose hopped down from the dish and waddled along the floor, with a knife and fork in its breast, to the little girl. Then the match went out and only the thick, damp, cold wall was before her. She lighted another match. Then she was sitting under a beautiful Christmas tree; it was greater and more ornamented than the one she had seen through the glass door at the rich merchant's. Thousands of candles burned upon the green branches, and colored pictures like those in the print shops looked down upon them. The little girl stretched forth her hand toward them; then the match went out. The Christmas lights mounted higher. She saw them now as stars in the sky; one of them fell down, forming a long line of fire.

"Now someone is dying," thought the little girl, for her

old grandmother, the only person who had loved her, and who was now dead, had told her that when a star fell down a soul mounted up to God.

She rubbed another match against the wall; it became bright again, and in the brightness the old grandmother stood clear and shining, mild and lovely.

"Grandmother!" cried the child. "Oh, take me with you! I know you will go when the match is burned out. You will vanish like the warm fire, the warm food, and the great, glorious Christmas tree!"

And she hastily rubbed the whole bundle of matches, for she wished to hold her grandmother fast. And the matches burned with such a glow that it became brighter than in the middle of the day; grandmother had never been so large or so beautiful. She took the little girl in her arms, and both flew in brightness and joy above the earth, very, very high, and up there was neither cold, nor hunger, nor care—they were with God.

But in the corner, leaning against the wall, sat the poor girl with red cheeks and smiling mouth, frozen to death on the last evening of the old year. The New Year's sun rose upon a little corpse! The child sat there, stiff and cold, with the matches, of which one bundle was burned. "She wanted to warm herself," the people said. No one imagined what a beautiful thing she had seen and in what glory she had gone in with her grandmother to the New Year's Day.

Three Kings of Orient

by JOHN HENRY HOPKINS

A Christmas Carol

We three kings of Orient are,
Bearing gifts we traverse afar,
    Field and Fountain,
    Moor and Mountain,
Following yonder Star.

Chorus

O Star of wonder, Star of Night,
Star with royal beauty bright,
    Westward leading,
    Still proceeding,
Guide us to Thy perfect light.

Gaspard

Born a king on Bethlehem plain,
Gold I bring to crown Him again,
    King for ever,
    Ceasing never
Over us all to reign.
          O Star . . .

Melchior

Frankincense to offer have I,
Incense owns a Deity nigh:

Three Kings of Orient

Prayer and praising
All men raising,
Worship Him God on High.
              O Star . . .

Balthasar

Myrrh is mine; its bitter perfume
Breathes a life of gathering gloom;
    Sorrowing, sighing,
    Bleeding, dying,
Sealed in the stone-cold tomb.

Glorious now behold Him arise,
King, and God, and Sacrifice;
    Heav'n sings
    Hallelujah: Hallelujah
The earth replies.

Chorus

O Star of wonder, Star of Night,
Star with royal beauty bright,
    Westward leading,
    Still proceeding,
Guide us to Thy perfect light.

The Gift of the Magi

by O. HENRY

ONE DOLLAR and eighty-seven cents. That was all. And sixty cents of it was in pennies. Pennies saved one and two at a time by bulldozing the grocer and the vegetable man and the butcher until one's cheeks burned with the silent imputation of parsimony that such close dealing implied. Three times Della counted it. One dollar and eighty-seven cents. And the next day would be Christmas.

There was clearly nothing to do but flop down on the shabby little couch and howl. So Della did it. Which instigates the moral reflection that life is made up of sobs, sniffles, and smiles, with sniffles predominating.

While the mistress of the home is gradually subsiding from the first stage to the second, take a look at the home. A furnished flat at $8 per week. It did not exactly beggar description, but it certainly had that word on the lookout for the mendicancy squad.

In the vestibule below was a letter-box into which no letter would go, and an electric button from which no mortal finger could coax a ring. Also appertaining thereunto was a card bearing the name "Mr. James Dillingham Young."

The "Dillingham" had been flung to the breeze during a former period of prosperity when its possessor was being paid $30 per week. Now, when the income was shrunk to $20, the letters of "Dillingham" looked blurred, as though they were thinking seriously of contracting to a modest and unassuming D. But whenever Mr. James Dillingham Young came home and reached his flat above he was called "Jim" and greatly hugged by Mrs. James Dillingham Young, already introduced to you as Della. Which is all very good.

Della finished her cry and attended to her cheeks with the powder rag. She stood by the window and looked out dully at a grey cat walking a grey fence in a grey backyard. To-morrow would be Christmas Day, and she had only $1.87 with which to buy Jim a present. She had been saving every penny she could for months, with this result. Twenty dollars a week doesn't go far. Expenses had been greater than she had calculated. They always are. Only $1.87 to buy a present for Jim. Her Jim. Many a happy hour she had spent planning for something nice for him. Something fine and rare and sterling —something just a little bit near to being worthy of the honour of being owned by Jim.

There was a pier-glass between the windows of the room. Perhaps you have seen a pier-glass in an $8 flat. A very thin and very agile person may, by observing his reflection in a rapid sequence of longitudinal strips, obtain a fairly accurate conception of his looks. Della, being slender, had mastered the art.

Suddenly she whirled from the window and stood before the glass. Her eyes were shining brilliantly, but her face had lost its colour within twenty seconds. Rapidly she pulled down her hair and let it fall to its full length.

Now, there were two possessions of the James Dillingham Youngs in which they both took a mighty pride. One was Jim's gold watch that had been his father's and grandfather's. The other was Della's hair. Had the Queen of Sheba lived in the flat across the airshaft, Della would have let her hair hang out the window some day to dry just to depreciate Her Majesty's jewels and gifts. Had King Solomon been the janitor, with all his treasures piled up in the basement, Jim would have pulled out his watch every time he passed, just to see him pluck at his beard from envy.

So now Della's beautiful hair fell about her, rippling and

shining like a cascade of brown waters. It reached below her knee and made itself almost a garment for her. And then she did it up again nervously and quickly. Once she faltered for a minute and stood still while a tear or two splashed on the worn red carpet.

On went her old brown jacket; on went her old brown hat. With a whirl of skirts and with the brilliant sparkle still in her eyes, she fluttered out the door and down the stairs to the street.

Where she stopped the sign read: "Mme. Sofronie. Hair Goods of All Kinds." One flight up Della ran, and collected herself, panting. Madame, large, too white, chilly, hardly looked the "Sofronie."

"Will you buy my hair?" asked Della.

"I buy hair," said Madame. "Take yer hat off and let's have a sight at the looks of it."

Down rippled the brown cascade.

"Twenty dollars," said Madame, lifting the mass with a practised hand.

"Give it to me quick," said Della.

Oh, and the next two hours tripped by on rosy wings. Forget the hashed metaphor. She was ransacking the stores for Jim's present.

She found it at last. It surely had been made for Jim and no one else. There was no other like it in any of the stores, and she had turned all of them inside out. It was a platinum fob chain simple and chaste in design, properly proclaiming its value by substance alone and not by meretricious ornamentation—as all good things should do. It was even worthy of The Watch. As soon as she saw it she knew that it must be Jim's. It was like him. Quietness and value—the description applied to both. Twenty-one dollars they took from her for it, and she hurried home with the 87 cents. With that chain on his watch Jim might be properly anxious about the time in any company. Grand as the watch was, he sometimes looked at it on the sly on account of the old leather strap that he used in place of a chain.

When Della reached home her intoxication gave way a little to prudence and reason. She got out her curling irons and lighted the gas and went to work repairing the ravages made by generosity added to love. Which is always a tremendous task, dear friends—a mammoth task.

Within forty minutes her head was covered with tiny, close-lying curls that made her look wonderfully like a truant schoolboy. She looked at her reflection in the mirror long, carefully, and critically.

"If Jim doesn't kill me," she said to herself, "before he takes a second look at me, he'll say I look like a Coney Island chorus girl. But what could I do—oh! what could I do with a dollar and eighty-seven cents?"

At 7 o'clock the coffee was made and the frying-pan was on the back of the stove hot and ready to cook the chops.

Jim was never late. Della doubled the fob chain in her hand and sat on the corner of the table near the door that he always entered. Then she heard his step on the stair away down on the first flight, and she turned white for just a moment. She had a habit of saying little silent prayers about the simplest everyday things, and now she whispered: "Please God, make him think I am still pretty."

The door opened and Jim stepped in and closed it. He looked thin and very serious. Poor fellow, he was only twenty-two—and to be burdened with a family! He needed a new overcoat and he was without gloves.

Jim stopped inside the door, as immovable as a setter at the scent of quail. His eyes were fixed upon Della, and there was an expression in them that she could not read, and it terrified her. It was not anger, nor surprise, nor disapproval, nor horror, nor any of the sentiments that she had been prepared for. He simply stared at her fixedly with that peculiar expression on his face.

Della wriggled off the table and went for him.

"Jim, darling," she cried, "don't look at me that way. I had my hair cut off and sold it because I couldn't have lived through Christmas without giving you a present. It'll grow out again—you won't mind, will you? I just had to do it. My hair grows awfully fast. Say 'Merry Christmas!' Jim, and let's be happy. You don't know what a nice—what a beautiful, nice gift I've got for you."

"You've cut off your hair?" asked Jim, laboriously, as if he had not arrived at that patent fact yet even after the hardest mental labour.

"Cut it off and sold it," said Della. "Don't you like me just as well, anyhow? I'm me without my hair, ain't I?"

Jim looked about the room curiously.

"You say your hair is gone?" he said, with an air almost of idiocy.

"You needn't look for it," said Della. "It's sold, I tell you—sold and gone, too. It's Christmas Eve, boy. Be good to me, for it went for you. Maybe the hairs of my head were numbered," she went on with a sudden serious sweetness, "but nobody could ever count my love for you. Shall I put the chops on, Jim?"

Out of his trance Jim seemed quickly to wake. He enfolded his Della. For ten seconds let us regard with discreet scrutiny some inconsequential object in the other direction. Eight dollars a week or a million a year—what is the difference? A mathematician or a wit would give you the wrong answer. The magi brought valuable gifts, but that was not among them. This dark assertion will be illuminated later on.

Jim drew a package from his overcoat pocket and threw it upon the table.

"Don't make any mistake, Dell," he said, "about me. I don't think there's anything in the way of a haircut or a shave or a shampoo that could make me like my girl any less. But if you'll unwrap that package you may see why you had me going a while at first."

White fingers and nimble tore at the string and paper. And then an ecstatic scream of joy; and then, alas! a quick feminine change to hysterical tears and wails, necessitating the immediate employment of all the comforting powers of the lord of the flat.

For there lay The Combs—the set of combs, side and back, that Della had worshipped for long in a Broadway window. Beautiful combs, pure tortoise shell, with jeweled rims—just the shade to wear in the beautiful vanished hair. They were expensive combs, she knew, and her heart had simply craved and yearned over them without the least hope of possession. And now, they were hers, but the tresses that should have adorned the coveted adornments were gone.

But she hugged them to her bosom, and at length she was able to look up with dim eyes and a smile and say: "My hair grows so fast, Jim!"

And then Della leaped up like a little singed cat and cried, "Oh, oh!"

Jim had not yet seen his beautiful present. She held it out to him eagerly upon her open palm. The dull precious metal seemed to flash with a reflection of her bright and ardent spirit.

"Isn't it a dandy, Jim? I hunted all over town to find it. You'll have to look at the time a hundred times a day now. Give me your watch. I want to see how it looks on it."

Instead of obeying, Jim tumbled down on the couch and put his hands under the back of his head and smiled.

"Dell," said he, "let's put our Christmas presents away and keep 'em a while. They're too nice to use just at present. I sold the watch to get the money to buy your combs. And now suppose you put the chops on."

The magi, as you know, were wise men—wonderfully wise men who brought gifts to the Babe in the manger. They invented the art of giving Christmas presents. Being wise, their gifts were no doubt wise ones, possibly bearing the privilege of exchange in case of duplication. And here I have lamely related to you the uneventful chronicle of two foolish children in a flat who most unwisely sacrificed for each other the greatest treasures of their house. But in a last word to the wise of these days let it be said that of all who give gifts these two were the wisest. Of all who give and receive gifts, such as they are wisest. Everywhere they are wisest. They are the magi.

Silent Night, Holy Night

by JOSEPH MOHR

Silent Night, Holy Night!
All is calm, all is bright,
'Round yon virgin mother and child!
Holy Infant, so tender and mild,
Sleep in heavenly peace.

Silent Night, Holy Night!
Shepherds quake at the sight!
Glories stream from heaven afar,
Heav'nly hosts sing Alleluia;
Christ, the Saviour is born.

Silent Night, Holy Night!
Son of God, love's pure light,
Radiant beams from Thy holy face,
With the dawn of redeeming grace
Jesus, Lord, at Thy birth.

Silent Night, Holy Night!
Guiding Star, lend thy light,
See the eastern wise men bring,
Gifts and homage to our King,
Jesus, the Saviour is born.

Christmas Every Day

(from *Christmas Every Day and Other Stories Told for Children*)

by WILLIAM DEAN HOWELLS

THE LITTLE GIRL came into her papa's study, as she always did
Saturday morning before breakfast, and asked for a story. He
tried to beg off that morning, for he was very busy, but she
would not let him. So he began:

"Well, once there was a little pig—"

She put her hand over his mouth and stopped him at the
word. She said she had heard little pig-stories till she was perfectly sick of them.

"Well, what kind of story *shall* I tell, then?"

"About Christmas. It's getting to be the season. It's past
Thanksgiving already."

"It seems to me," her papa argued, "that I've told as often
about Christmas as I have about little pigs."

"No difference! Christmas is more interesting."

"Well!" Her papa roused himself from his writing by a
great effort. "Well, then, I'll tell you about the little girl that
wanted it Christmas every day in the year. How would you
like that?"

"First-rate!" said the little girl; and she nestled into comfortable shape in his lap, ready for listening.

"Very well, then, this little pig— Oh, what are you pound-
ing me for?"

"Because you said little pig instead of little girl."

"I should like to know what's the difference between a little pig and a little girl that wanted it Christmas every day!"

"Papa," said the little girl, warningly, "if you don't go on, I'll *give* it to you!" And at this her papa darted off like lightning, and began to tell the story as fast as he could.

Well, once there was a little girl who liked Christmas so much that she wanted it to be Christmas every day in the year; and as soon as Thanksgiving was over she began to send postal-cards to the old Christmas Fairy to ask if she mightn't have it. But the old Fairy never answered any of the postals; and after a while the little girl found out that the Fairy was pretty particular, and wouldn't notice anything but letters—not even correspondence cards in envelopes; but real letters on sheets of paper, and sealed outside with a monogram—or your initial, anyway. So, then, she began to send her letters; and in about three weeks—or just the day before Christmas, it was—she got a letter from the Fairy, saying she might have it Christmas every day for a year, and then they would see about having it longer.

The little girl was a good deal excited already, preparing for the old-fashioned, once-a-year Christmas that was coming the next day, and perhaps the Fairy's promise didn't make such an impression on her as it would have made at some other time. She just resolved to keep it to herself, and surprise everybody with it as it kept coming true; and then it slipped out of her mind altogether.

She had a splendid Christmas. She went to bed early, so as to let Santa Claus have a chance at the stockings, and in the morning she was up the first of anybody and went and felt them, and found hers all lumpy with packages of candy, and oranges and grapes, and pocketbooks and rubber balls, and all kinds of small presents, and her big brother's with nothing but the tongs in them, and her young lady sister's with a new silk umbrella, and her papa's and mamma's with potatoes and pieces of coal wrapped up in tissue-paper, just as they always had every Christmas. Then she waited around till the rest of the family were up, and she was the first to burst into the library, when the doors were opened, and look at the large presents laid out on the library-table—books, and portfolios, and boxes of stationery, and breastpins, and dolls, and little stoves, and dozens of handkerchiefs, and inkstands, and skates, and snow-shovels, and photograph-frames, and little easels, and boxes of water-colors, and Turkish paste, and nougat, and candied cherries, and dolls' houses, and waterproofs —and the big Christmas-tree, lighted and standing in a wastebasket in the middle.

She had a splendid Christmas all day. She ate so much candy that she did not want any breakfast; and the whole forenoon the presents kept pouring in that the expressman had not had time to deliver the night before; and she went round giving the presents she had got for other people, and came home and ate turkey and cranberry for dinner, and plum-pudding and nuts and raisins and oranges and more candy, and then went out and coasted, and came in with a stomach-ache, crying; and her papa said he would see if his house was turned into that sort of fool's paradise another year; and they had a light supper, and pretty early everybody went to bed cross.

Here the little girl pounded her papa in the back, again.

"Well, what now? Did I say pigs?"

"You made them *act* like pigs."

"Well, didn't they?"

"No matter; you oughtn't to put it into a story."

"Very well, then, I'll take it all out."

Her father went on:

The little girl slept very heavily, and she slept very late, but she was wakened at last by the other children dancing round her bed with their stockings full of presents in their hands.

"What is it?" said the little girl, and she rubbed her eyes and tried to rise up in bed.

"Christmas! Christmas! Christmas!" they all shouted, and waved their stockings.

"Nonsense! It was Christmas yesterday."

Her brothers and sisters just laughed. "We don't know about that. It's Christmas to-day, anyway. You come into the library and see."

Then all at once it flashed on the little girl that the Fairy was keeping her promise, and her year of Christmases was beginning. She was dreadfully sleepy, but she sprang up like a lark—a lark that had overeaten itself and gone to bed cross—and darted into the library. There it was again! Books, and portfolios, and boxes of stationery, and breastpins—

"You needn't go over it all, papa; I guess I can remember just what was there," said the little girl.

Well, and there was the Christmas-tree blazing away, and the family picking out their presents, but looking pretty sleepy, and her father perfectly puzzled, and her mother ready to cry. "I'm sure I don't see how I'm to dispose of all these things," said her mother, and her father said it seemed to him they had had something just like it the day before, but he supposed he must have dreamed it. This struck the little girl as the best kind of a joke; and so she ate so much candy she didn't want any breakfast, and went round carrying presents, and had turkey and cranberry for dinner, and then went out and coasted, and came in with a—

"Papa!"

"Well, what now?"

"What did you promise, you forgetful thing?"

"Oh! oh yes!"

Well, the next day, it was just the same thing over again, but everybody getting crosser; and at the end of a week's time so many people had lost their tempers that you could pick up lost tempers anywhere; they perfectly strewed the ground. Even when people tried to recover their tempers they usually got somebody else's, and it made the most dreadful mix.

The little girl began to get frightened, keeping the secret all to herself; she wanted to tell her mother, but she didn't dare to; and she was ashamed to ask the Fairy to take back her gift, it seemed ungrateful and ill-bred, and she thought she would try to stand it, but she hardly knew how she could, for a whole year. So it went on and on, and it was Christmas on St. Valentine's Day and Washington's Birthday, just the same as any day, and it didn't skip even the First of April, though everything was counterfeit that day, and that was some *little* relief.

After a while coal and potatoes began to be awfully scarce, so many had been wrapped up in tissue-paper to fool papas and mammas with. Turkeys got to be about a thousand dollars apiece—

"Papa!"

"Well, what?"

"You're beginning to fib."

"Well, *two* thousand, then."

And they got to passing off almost anything for turkeys— half-grown humming-birds, and even rocs out of the *Arabian Nights*—the real turkeys were so scarce. And cranberries— well, they asked a diamond apiece for cranberries. All the woods and orchards were cut down for Christmas-trees, and where the woods and orchards used to be it looked just like a stubble-field, with the stumps. After a while they had to make Christmas-trees out of rags, and stuff them with bran, like old-fashioned dolls; but there were plenty of rags, because people got so poor, buying presents for one another, that they couldn't get any new clothes, and they just wore their old ones to tatters. They got so poor that everybody had to go to the poor-house, except the confectioners, and the fancy-store keepers, and the picture-book sellers, and the expressmen; and *they* all got so rich and proud that they would hardly wait upon a person when he came to buy. It was perfectly shameful!

Well, after it had gone on about three or four months, the little girl, whenever she came into the room in the morning and saw those great ugly, lumpy stockings dangling at the fire-place, and the disgusting presents around everywhere, used to just sit down and burst out crying. In six months she was perfectly exhausted; she couldn't even cry any more; she just lay on the lounge and rolled her eyes and panted. About the beginning of October she took to sitting down on dolls wherever she found them—French dolls, or any kind—she hated the sight of them so; and by Thanksgiving she was crazy, and just slammed her presents across the room.

By that time people didn't carry presents around nicely any more. They flung them over the fence, or through the window, or anything; and, instead of running their tongues out and taking great pains to write "For dear Papa," or "Mamma," or "Brother," or "Sister," or "Susie," or "Sammie," or "Billie," or "Bobbie," or "Jimmie," or "Jennie," or whoever it was, and troubling to get the spelling right, and then signing their names, and "Xmas, 18—," they used to write in the gift-books, "Take it, you horrid old thing!" and then go and bang it against the front door. Nearly everybody had built barns to hold their presents, but pretty soon the barns overflowed, and then they used to let them lie out in the rain, or anywhere. Sometimes the police used to come and tell them to shovel their presents off the sidewalk, or they would arrest them.

"I thought you said everybody had gone to the poor-house," interrupted the little girl.

"They did go, at first," said her papa; "but after a while the poor-houses got so full that they had to send the people back to their own houses. They tried to cry, when they got back, but they couldn't make the least sound."

"Why couldn't they?"

"Because they had lost their voices, saying 'Merry Christmas' so much. Did I tell you how it was on the Fourth of July?"

"No; how was it?" And the little girl nestled closer, in expectation of something uncommon.

Well, the night before, the boys stayed up to celebrate, as they always do, and fell asleep before twelve o'clock, as usual, expecting to be wakened by the bells and cannon. But it was nearly eight o'clock before the first boy in the United States woke up, and then he found out what the trouble was. As soon as he could get his clothes on he ran out of the house and smashed a big cannon-torpedo down on the pavement; but it didn't make any more noise than a damp wad of paper; and after he tried about twenty or thirty more, he began to pick them up and look at them. Every single torpedo was a big raisin! Then he just streaked it upstairs, and examined his firecrackers and toy pistol and two-dollar collection of fireworks, and found that they were nothing but sugar and candy painted up to look like fireworks! Before ten o'clock every boy in the United States found out that his Fourth of July things had turned into Christmas things; and then they just sat down and cried—they were so mad. There are about twenty million boys in the United States, and so you can imagine what a noise they made. Some men got together before night, with a little powder that hadn't turned into purple sugar yet, and they said they would fire off *one* cannon, anyway. But the cannon burst into a thousand pieces, for it was nothing but rock-candy, and some of the men nearly got killed. The Fourth of July orations all turned into Christmas carols, and when anybody tried to read the Declaration, instead of saying, "When in the course of human events it becomes necessary," he was sure to sing, "God rest you, merry gentlemen." It was perfectly awful.

The little girl drew a deep sigh of satisfaction.

"And how was it at Thanksgiving?"

Her papa hesitated. "Well, I'm almost afraid to tell you. I'm afraid you'll think it's wicked."

"Well, tell, anyway," said the little girl.

Well, before it came Thanksgiving it had leaked out who had caused all these Christmases. The little girl had suffered so much that she had talked about it in her sleep; and after that hardly anybody would play with her. People just perfectly despised her, because if it had not been for her greediness it wouldn't have happened; and now, when it came Thanksgiving, and she wanted them to go to church, and have squash-pie and turkey, and show their gratitude, they said that all the turkeys had been eaten up for her old Christmas dinners, and if she would stop the Christmases, they would see about the gratitude. Wasn't it dreadful? And the very next day the little girl began to send letters to the Christmas Fairy, and then telegrams, to stop it. But it didn't do any good; and then she got to calling at the Fairy's house, but the girl that came to the door always said, "Not at home," or "Engaged," or "At dinner," or something like that; and so it went on till it came to the old once-a-year Christmas Eve. The little girl fell asleep, and when she woke up in the morning—

"She found it was all nothing but a dream," suggested the little girl.

"No, indeed!" said her papa. "It was all every bit true!"

"Well, what *did* she find out, then?"

"Why, that it wasn't Christmas at last, and wasn't ever going to be, any more. Now it's time for breakfast."

The little girl held her papa fast around the neck.

"You sha'n't go if you're going to leave it *so!*"

"How do you want it left?"

"Christmas once a year."

"All right," said her papa; and he went on again.

Well, there was the greatest rejoicing all over the country, and it extended clear up into Canada. The people met together everywhere, and kissed and cried for joy. The city carts went around and gathered up all the candy and raisins and nuts, and dumped them into the river; and it made the fish perfectly sick; and the whole United States, as far out as Alaska, was one blaze of bonfires, where the children were burning up their gift-books and presents of all kinds. They had the greatest *time!*

The little girl went to thank the old Fairy because she had stopped its being Christmas, and she said she hoped she would keep her promise and see that Christmas never, never came again. Then the Fairy frowned, and asked her if she was sure she knew what she meant; and the little girl asked her, Why not? and the old Fairy said that now she was behaving just as greedily as ever, and she'd better look out. This made the little girl think it all over carefully again, and she said she would be willing to have it Christmas about once in a thousand years; and then she said a hundred, and then she said ten, and at last she got down to one. Then the Fairy said that was the good old way that had pleased people ever since Christmas began, and she was agreed. Then the little girl said, "What're your shoes made of?" And the Fairy said, "Leather." And the little girl said, "Bargain's done forever," and skipped off, and hippity-hopped the whole way home, she was so glad.

"How will that do?" asked the papa.

"First-rate!" said the little girl; but she hated to have the story stop, and was rather sober.

However, her mamma put her head in at the door, and asked her papa, "Are you never coming to breakfast? What have you been telling that child?"

"Oh, just a moral tale."

The little girl caught him around the neck again.

"*We* know! Don't you tell *what*, papa! Don't you tell *what!*"

Christmas and New Year Bells

by ALFRED TENNYSON

The time draws near the birth of Christ:
   The moon is hid; the night is still;
   The Christmas bells from hill to hill
Answer each other in the mist.

Four voices of four hamlets round,
   From far and near, on mead and moor,
   Swell out and fail, as if a door
Were shut between me and the sound:

Each voice four changes on the wind,
   That now dilate, and now decrease,
   Peace and goodwill, goodwill and peace,
Peace and goodwill, to all mankind.

This year I slept and woke with pain,
   I almost wish'd no more to wake,
   And that my hold on life would break
Before I heard those bells again:

But they the troubled spirit rule,
   For they controll'd me when a boy;
   They bring me sorrow touch'd with joy,
The merry, merry bells of Yule.

Ring out, wild bells, to the wild sky,
   The flying cloud, the frosty light:

The year is dying in the night;
Ring out, wild bells, and let him die.

Ring out the old, ring in the new,
  Ring, happy bells, across the snow:
  The year is going, let him go;
Ring out the false, ring in the true.

Ring out the grief that saps the mind,
  For those that here we see no more;
  Ring out the feud of rich and poor,
Ring in redress to all mankind.

Ring out a slowly dying cause,
  And ancient forms of party strife;
  Ring in the nobler modes of life,
With sweeter manners, purer laws.

Ring out the want, the care, the sin,
  The faithless coldness of the times;
  Ring out, ring out my mournful rhymes,
But ring the fuller minstrel in.

Ring out false pride in place and blood,
  The civic slander and the spite;
  Ring in the love of truth and right,
Ring in the common love of good.

Ring out old shapes of foul disease,
  Ring out the narrowing lust of gold;
  Ring out the thousand wars of old
Ring in the thousand years of peace.

Christmas and New Year Bells

Ring in the valiant man and free,
  The larger heart, the kindlier hand;
  Ring out the darkness of the land,
Ring in the Christ that is to be.

Down Pens

(from *The Complete Saki* by H. H. Munro)

by SAKI

"Have you written to thank the Froplinsons for what they sent us?" asked Egbert.

"No," said Janetta, with a note of tired defiance in her voice; "I've written eleven letters today expressing surprise and gratitude for sundry unmerited gifts, but I haven't written to the Froplinsons."

"Someone will have to write to them," said Egbert.

"I don't dispute the necessity, but I don't think the someone should be me," said Janetta. "I wouldn't mind writing a letter of angry recrimination or heartless satire to some suitable recipient; in fact, I should rather enjoy it, but I've come to the end of my capacity for expressing servile amiability. Eleven letters today and nine yesterday, all couched in the same strain of ecstatic thankfulness: really, you can't expect me to sit down to another. There is such a thing as writing oneself out."

"I've written nearly as many," said Egbert, "and I've had my usual business correspondence to get through too. Besides, I don't know what it was that the Froplinsons sent us."

"A William the Conqueror calendar," said Janetta, "with a quotation of one of his great thoughts for every day in the year."

"Impossible," said Egbert; "he didn't have three hundred and sixty-five thoughts in the whole of his life, or, if he did, he kept them to himself. He was a man of action, not of introspection."

"Well, it was William Wordsworth, then," said Janetta; "I know William came into it somewhere."

"That sounds more probable," said Egbert; "well, let's collaborate on this letter of thanks and get it done. I'll dictate, and you can scribble it down. 'Dear Mrs. Froplinson—thank you and your husband so much for the very pretty calendar you sent us. It was very good of you to think of us.'"

"You can't possibly say that," said Janetta, laying down her pen.

"It's what I always do say, and what everyone says to me," protested Egbert.

"We sent them something on the twenty-second," said Janetta, "so they simply had to think of us. There was no getting away from it."

"What did we send them?" asked Egbert gloomily.

"Bridge-markers," said Janetta, "in a cardboard case, with some inanity about 'digging for fortune with a royal spade' emblazoned on the cover. The moment I saw it in the shop I said to myself 'Froplinsons' and to the attendant 'How much?' When he said 'Ninepence!' I gave him their address, jabbed our card in, paid tenpence or elevenpence to cover the postage, and thanked heaven. With less sincerity and infinitely more trouble they eventually thanked me."

"The Froplinsons don't play bridge," said Egbert.

"One is not supposed to notice social deformities of that sort," said Janetta; "it wouldn't be polite. Besides, what trouble did they take to find out whether we read Wordsworth with gladness? For all they knew or cared we might be frantically embedded in the belief that all poetry begins and ends with John Masefield, and it might infuriate or depress us to have a daily sample of Wordsworthian products flung at us."

"Well, let's get on with the letter of thanks," said Egbert.

"Proceed," said Janetta.

" 'How clever of you to guess that Wordsworth is our favourite poet,' " dictated Egbert.

Again Janetta laid down her pen.

"Do you realize what that means?" she asked; "a Wordsworth booklet next Christmas, and another calendar the Christmas after, with the same problem of having to write suitable letters of thankfulness. No, the best thing to do is to drop all further allusion to the calendar and switch off on to some other topic."

"But what other topic?"

"Oh, something like this: 'What do you think of the New Year Honours List? A friend of ours made such a clever remark when he read it.' Then you can stick in any remark that comes into your head; it needn't be clever. The Froplinsons won't know whether it is or isn't."

"We don't even know on which side they are in politics," objected Egbert; "and anyhow you can't suddenly dismiss the subject of the calendar. Surely there must be some intelligent remark that can be made about it."

"Well, we can't think of one," said Janetta wearily; "the fact is, we've both written ourselves out. Heavens! I've just remembered Mrs. Stephen Ludberry. I haven't thanked her for what she sent."

"What did she send?"

"I forget; I think it was a calendar."

There was a long silence, the forlorn silence of those who are bereft of hope and have almost ceased to care.

Presently Egbert started from his seat with an air of resolution. The light of battle was in his eyes.

"Let me come to the writing table," he exclaimed.

"Gladly," said Janetta. "Are you going to write to Mrs. Ludberry or the Froplinsons?"

"To neither," said Egbert, drawing a stack of note-paper towards him; "I'm going to write to the editor of every enlightened and influential newspaper in the Kingdom. I'm going to suggest that there should be a sort of epistolary Truce of God during the festivities of Christmas and New Year. From the twenty-fourth of December to the third or fourth of January it shall be considered an offence against good sense and good feeling to write or expect any letter or communication that does not deal with the necessary events of the moment. Answers to invitations, arrangements about trains, renewal of club subscriptions, and, of course, all the ordinary everyday affairs of business, sickness, engaging new cooks, and so forth, these will be dealt with in the usual manner as something inevitable, a legitimate part of our daily life. But all the devastating accretions of correspondence, incident to the festive season, these should be swept away to give the season a chance of being really festive, a time of untroubled, unpunctuated peace and good will."

"But you would have to make some acknowledgment of presents received," objected Janetta; "otherwise people would never know whether they had arrived safely."

"Of course, I have thought of that," said Egbert; "every present that was sent off would be accompanied by a ticket bearing the date of dispatch and the signature of the sender, and some conventional hieroglyphic to show that it was intended to be a Christmas or New Year gift; there would be a counterfoil with space for the recipient's name and the date of arrival, and all you would have to do would be to sign and date the counterfoil, add a conventional hieroglyphic indicating heartfelt thanks and gratified surprise, put the thing into an envelope and post it."

"It sounds delightfully simple," said Janetta wistfully, "but people would consider it too cut-and-dried, too perfunctory."

"It is not a bit more perfunctory than the present system," said Egbert; "I have only the same conventional language of gratitude at my disposal with which to thank dear old Colonel Chuttle for his perfectly delicious Stilton, which we shall devour to the last morsel, and the Froplinsons know that we are bored with their calendar, whatever we may say to the contrary, just as we know that they are bored with the bridge-markers in spite of their written assurance that they thanked us for our charming little gift. What is more, the Colonel knows that even if we had taken a sudden aversion to Stilton or been forbidden it by the doctor, we should still have written a letter of hearty thanks around it. So you see the present system of acknowledgment is just as perfunctory as the counterfoil business would be, only ten times more tiresome and brain-racking."

"Your plan would certainly bring the ideal of a Happy Christmas a step nearer realization," said Janetta.

"There are exceptions, of course," said Egbert, "people who really try to infuse a breath of reality into their letters of acknowledgment. Aunt Susan, for instance, who writes: 'Thank you very much for the ham; not such a good flavor as the one you sent last year, which itself was not a particularly good one. Hams are not what they used to be.' It would be a pity to be deprived of her Christmas comments, but that loss would be swallowed up in the general gain."

"Meanwhile," said Janetta, "what *am* I to say to the Froplinsons?"

Christmas in a Village

(from *The Shepherd's Calendar*)

by JOHN CLARE

Each house is swept the day before,
And windows stuck with evergreens;
The snow is besomed from the door,
And comfort crowns the cottage scenes.
Gilt holly with its thorny pricks
And yew and box with berries small,
These deck the unused candlesticks,
And pictures hanging by the wall.

Neighbours resume their annual cheer,
Wishing with smiles and spirits high
Glad Christmas and a happy year
To every morning passer-by.
Milkmaids their Christmas journeys go
Accompanied with favoured swain,
And children pace the crumping snow
To taste their granny's cake again.

Hung with the ivy's veining bough,
The ash trees round the cottage farm
Are often stripped of branches now
The cottar's Christmas hearth to warm.
He swings and twists his hazel band,
And lops them off with sharpened hook,
And oft brings ivy in his hand
To decorate the chimney nook . . .

Christmas in a Village

The shepherd now no more afraid
Since custom doth the chance bestow
Starts up to kiss the giggling maid
Beneath the branch of mistletoe
That 'neath each cottage beam is seen
With pearl-like berries shining gay,
The shadow still of what hath been
Which fashion yearly fades away.

And singers too, a merry throng,
At early morn with simple skill
Yet imitate the angel's song
And chant their Christmas ditty still;
And 'mid the storm that dies and swells
By fits—in hummings softly steals
The music of the village bells
Ringing round their merry peals.

And when it's past, a merry crew
Bedecked in masks and ribbons gay,
The morris dance their sports renew
And act their winter evening play.
The clown turned king for penny praise
Storms with the actor's strut and swell,
And harlequin a laugh to raise
Wears his hunchback and tinkling bell.

And oft for pence and spicy ale
With winter nosegays pinned before,
The wassail singer tells her tale
And drawls her Christmas carols o'er,
While prentice boy with ruddy face
And rime-bepowdered dancing locks
From door to door with happy pace
Runs round to claim his Christmas box.

Christmas with Sir Roger

(*The Spectator, No. 269*)

by JOSEPH ADDISON

I WAS this morning surprised with a great knocking at the door, when my landlady's daughter came up to me and told me there was a man below desired to speak with me. Upon my asking who it was, she told me it was a very grave elderly person, but that she did not know his name. I immediately went down to him, and found him to be the coachman of my worthy friend, Sir Roger de Coverley. He told me that his master came to town last night, and would be glad to take a turn with me in Gray's-Inn walks. As I was wondering in myself what had brought Sir Roger to town, not having lately received any letter from him, he told me that his master was come up to get a sight of Prince Eugene, and that he desired I would immediately meet him.

I was not a little pleased with the curiosity of the old knight, though I did not much wonder at it, having heard him say more than once in private discourse, that he looked upon Prince Eugenio (for so the knight always calls him) to be a greater man than Scanderbeg.

I was no sooner come into Gray's-Inn walks, but I heard my friend upon the terrace hemming twice or thrice to himself with great vigor, for he loves to clear his pipes in good air (to make use of his own phrase), and is not a little pleased with anyone who takes notice of the strength which he still exerts in his morning hems.

I was touched with a secret joy at the sight of the good old man, who before he saw me was engaged in conversation with a beggarman that had asked an alms of him. I could hear my friend chide him for not finding out some work; but at the same time saw him put his hand in his pocket and give him sixpence.

Our salutations were very hearty on both sides, consisting of many kind shakes of the hand, and several affectionate looks which we cast upon one another. After which the knight told me my good friend his chaplain was very well, and much at my service, and that the Sunday before he had made a most incomparable sermon out of Dr. Barrow. "I have left," says he, "all my affairs in his hands, and being willing to lay an obligation upon him, have deposited with him thirty marks, to be distributed among his poor parishioners."

He then proceeded to acquaint me with the welfare of Will Wimble. Upon which he put his hand into his fob and presented me in his name with a tobacco-stopper, telling me that Will had been busy all the beginning of the winter in turning great quantities of them; and that he made a present of one to every gentleman in the country who has good principles, and smokes. He added that poor Will was at present under great tribulation, for that Tom Touchy had taken the law of him for cutting some hazel sticks out of one of his hedges.

Among other pieces of news which the knight brought from his country-seat, he informed me that Moll White was dead, and that about a month after her death the wind was so very high that it blew down the end of one of his barns. "But for my own part," says Sir Roger, "I do not think that the old woman had any hand in it."

He afterward fell into an account of the diversions which had passed in his house during the holidays; for Sir Roger, after the laudable custom of his ancestors, always keeps open house at Christmas. I learned from him that he had killed eight fat hogs for the season, that he had dealt about his chines very liberally among his neighbors, and that in particular he had sent a string of hog's-puddings with a pack of cards to every poor family in the parish. "I have often thought," says Sir Roger, "it happens very well that Christmas should fall out in the middle of the winter. It is the most dead uncomfortable time of the year, when the poor people would suffer very much from their poverty and cold, if they had not good cheer, warm fires, and Christmas gambols to support them. I love to rejoice their poor hearts at this season, and to see the whole village merry in my great hall. I allow a double quantity of malt to my small-beer, and set it a-running for twelve days to everyone that calls for it. I have always a piece of cold beef and a mince pie upon the table, and am wonderfully pleased to see my tenants pass away a whole evening in playing their innocent tricks and smutting one another. Our friend Will Wimble is as merry as any of them, and shows a thousand roguish tricks upon these occasions."

I was very much delighted with the reflection of my old friend, which carried so much goodness in it. He then launched out into the praise of the late act of Parliament for securing the Church of England, and told me with great satisfaction that he believed it already began to take effect, for that a rigid dissenter who chanced to dine at his house on Christmas Day had been observed to eat very plentifully of his plum porridge.

After having dispatched all our country matters, Sir Roger made several inquiries concerning the club, and particularly of his old antagonist, Sir Andrew Freeport. He asked me with a kind of smile whether Sir Andrew had not taken advantage of his absence to vent among them some of his republican doctrines; but soon after gathering up his countenance into a more than ordinary seriousness, "Tell me truly," says he, "don't you think Sir Andrew had a hand in the pope's procession?"—But without giving me time to answer him, "Well,

well," says he, "I know you are a wary man, and do not care to talk of public matters."

The knight then asked me if I had seen Prince Eugenio, and made me promise to get him a stand in some convenient place where he might have a full sight of that extraordinary man, whose presence does so much honor to the British nation. He dwelt very long on the praises of this great general, and I found that since I was with him in the country he had drawn many observations together out of his reading in Baker's Chronicle, and other authors, who always lie in his hall window, which very much redound to the honor of the prince.

Having passed away the greatest part of the morning in hearing the knight's reflections, which were partly private and partly political, he asked me if I would smoke a pipe with him over a dish of coffee at Squire's? As I love the old man, I take delight in complying with everything that is agreeable to him, and accordingly waited on him to the coffeehouse, where his venerable figure drew upon us the eyes of the whole room. He had no sooner seated himself at the upper end of the high table, but he called for a clean pipe, a paper of tobacco, a dish of coffee, a wax candle, and the Supplement, with such an air of cheerfulness and good humor, that all the boys in the coffeeroom (who seemed to take pleasure in serving him) were at once employed on his several errands, insomuch that nobody else could come at a dish of tea, until the knight had got all his conveniences about him.

The Sheep Herd

by SISTER MARIELLA

I am a shepherd—I have hated
The smell of damp sheep in the rain,
The pain
Of clouted shoes on weary feet,
The silly barking of watchdogs in the night,
The blinding light
Of summer suns on hillsides without shade.
Nor anything I did not wish was not
From hoar-frost on the meadow grass
To dizzy stars that blinked on stupidly and bright.

Last night
I went with other men who tended sheep
Over to Bethlehem to see—
We did not know just what we'd come to see
Who'd followed up a cloud of singing wings.
Until we came to where a young girl held
A little baby on her lap and smiled.

She made me think of flowers,
White flowers on long stems and blue night skies.
Nothing happened—
But today
I have been shaken with the joy
Of seeing hoar-frost wings
Atilt upon tall grasses; the sun
Upon the sheep, making their gray backs white

And silvery
Has hurt me with its beauty, and I heard
The sound of the barking watchdogs break
The tolling bells against the quiet hills.

I Take Supper with My Wife

by ANTOINE GUSTAVE DROZ

It was Christmas Eve, and a devilishly cold night. The snow fell in great flakes, which the wind beat against the window-panes. The distant chimes reached us, confused and faint through the heavy, cottony atmosphere. The passers-by, muffled in their cloaks, glided along hurriedly, brushing by the walls of the houses, bending their heads before the wind. Wrapped in my dressing gown, I smiled as I drummed on the windowpane, smiled at the passers-by, at the north wind and the snow, with the smile of a happy man who is in a warm room with his feet in a pair of flannel-lined slippers which sink into a thick, soft carpet.

My wife sat in a corner of the hearth with a great piece of cloth before her which she cut and trimmed off; and every now and then she raised her eyes, which met mine. A new book lay on the mantelpiece awaiting me, and a log in the fireplace whistled as it spit out those little blue flames which tempt one to poke it.

"There is nothing so stupid as a man trudging along in the snow. Is there?" said I.

"Sh-h-h!" said my wife, laying down her scissors. Then she stroked her chin thoughtfully with her tapering pink fingers, slightly plump at the extremities, and looked over very carefully the pieces she had just cut out.

"I say that it is absurd to go out into the cold when it is so easy to stay at home by the fire."

"Sh-h-h!"

"What the deuce are you doing that is so important?"

"I—I am cutting out a pair of suspenders for you"; and she resumed her task. Her hair was coiled a little higher than usual; and where I stood, behind her, I could just see, as she leaned over her work, the nape of her neck, white and velvety. Innumerable soft little locks curled there gracefully, and this pretty down reminded me of those ripe peaches into which we drive our teeth greedily. I leaned nearer to see and—kissed my wife on the neck.

"Monsieur!" exclaimed Louise, turning suddenly around.

"Madame!" and we both burst into a laugh.

"Come, come; on Christmas Eve!"

"Monsieur apologizes?"

"Madame complains?"

"Yes, madame complains. Madame complains of your not being more moved, more thrilled by the spirit of Christmas. The ding-ding-dong from the bells of Notre Dame awakens no emotion in you; and when the magic lantern went by under your very window, you were perfectly unmoved, utterly indifferent. I watched you attentively, though I pretended to work."

"Unmoved? Indifferent? I? When the magic lantern went by! Ah, my dear! you judge me very severely, and really—"

"Yes, yes; laugh if you will. It is nevertheless true that the pretty memories of your childhood are lost."

"Come, my pet, would you like me to stand my boots in the fireplace tonight before I go to bed? Would you like me to stop the magic-lantern man and go and get him a sheet and a candle end, as my mother used to do? I can almost see her as she handed him the sheet. 'Be careful you don't tear it, now,' she would say; and we all clapped our hands in the mysterious obscurity. I remember all those joys, dear; but, you see, so many things have happened since. Other pleasures have obliterated those."

"Yes, I understand—the pleasures of your bachelorhood! Come, now, I am sure this is the first Christmas Eve that has ever found you by your own fireside, in your dressing gown and without a supper, because you always had supper; that goes without saying—"

"Why, I don't know—"

"Yes, yes; I wager you always had a supper."

"Well, perhaps I did, once or twice, although I scarcely remember. I may have had supper with a few old friends. And what did it all amount to? Two pennies' worth of chestnuts and—"

"And a glass of sugar and water."

"Well, just about. Oh, it was nothing much, I can assure you! It sounds great at a distance. We talked awhile, and then we went to bed."

"And he says all that with the straightest face! You have never breathed a word of these simple pleasures to me."

"But, my dear, what I tell you is the absolute truth. I remember once, however, at Ernest's, when I was in rather high spirits, we had a little music afterwards— Will you push me that log? Well, never mind; it is almost midnight, and time for all reasonable people to—"

(Louise, rising and throwing her arms around me.) "Well, I don't choose to be reasonable, and I mean to eclipse the memory of those penny chestnuts and all that sugar and water!" (Pushing me hastily into my study and locking the door.)

"What the deuce is the matter with you, my dear?" I cried from the other side of the partition.

"Give me ten minutes, no more. Your paper is on the mantelpiece; you have not seen it tonight. You will find the matches in the corner."

Then I heard the rattle of china, the rustle of silky stuffs. Could my wife have gone crazy? At the end of about ten minutes she unlocked the door.

"Don't scold me for shutting you out," said she, embracing me. "Look at me. Have I not made myself beautiful? See! My hair just as you like it, high, and my neck uncovered. But my poor neck is so extremely shy that it never could have displayed itself in the broad light, if I had not encouraged it a little by wearing a low-necked gown. After all, it is only right to be in full-dress uniform at a supper with the authority."

"What supper?"

"Why, our supper. My supper with you, of course. Don't you see my illumination and the table covered with flowers and good things to eat? I had it all ready in the alcove; but, you see, to push the table before the fire and make something of a toilet, I had to be alone. I have a big drop of old Chambertin for you. Come, monsieur, come to supper; I am as hungry as a bear! May I offer you this chicken wing?"

"This is a charming idea of yours, my love, but I really feel ashamed of myself—in my dressing gown."

"Take it off, sir, if you are uncomfortable, but do not leave me with this chicken wing on my hands. Wait a minute; I want to wait upon you myself." And rising, she swung her napkin over her arm and pulled up her sleeve to her elbow. "Isn't that the way the waiters do at the restaurants, tell me?"

"Exactly. But stop a moment, waiter; will you permit me to kiss your hand?"

"I haven't time," she said, smiling, and she drove the corkscrew bravely into the neck of a bottle. "Chambertin—a pretty name! And, besides, do you remember, before we were married—*sapristi*, what a hard cork!—you told me you liked it on account of a play by Alfred de Musset?—which you never gave me to read, by the way. Do you see those little Bohemian glass tumblers that I bought especially for tonight? We will drink each other's health in them."

"And his too, eh?"

"The heir's, you mean? Poor little love of an heir, I should think so! Then I shall hide the two glasses and bring them out again this day next year, eh, dear? They will be the Christmas supper glasses, and we will have supper every year before the hearth, you and I alone, until our very old, old age."

"Yes; but when we shall have lost all our teeth—"

"Never mind; we shall have nice little soups, and it will nonetheless be very sweet. Another piece for me, please, with a little jelly, thank you."

As she held out her plate to me, I caught a glimpse of her arm, the pretty contours of which disappeared in the lace.

"What are you looking up my sleeve for instead of eating?"

"I am looking at your arm, dear. You are exquisitely pretty tonight; do you know it? Your hair is wonderfully becoming, and that gown—I had never seen that gown before."

"*Dame!* When a person starts out to make a conquest!"

"You are adorable!"

"Are you quite sure that I am adorable tonight, charming, ravishing?" Then, looking at her bracelet attentively, "In that case I don't see why—I don't see—"

"What is it that you don't see, dear?"

"I don't see why you don't come and kiss me."

And as the kiss was prolonged, she threw her head back, showing the double row of her pretty white teeth, exclaiming between her peals of laughter, "Give me some more *pâté!* I want some more *pâté!* Take care! You are going to break my Bohemian glass, the fruit of my economy! There is always some disaster when you try to kiss me. You remember at Madame de Brill's ball, two nights before we were married, how you tore my gown while we were waltzing in the little parlor?"

"Well, but it is very difficult to do two things at once—keep time with the music and kiss your partner."

"I remember when mamma asked me how I tore my gown, I felt that I was blushing up to the roots of my hair. And Madame D., that old yellow witch, said to me with her lenten smile, 'What a brilliant color you have tonight, my child!' I could have choked her! I said I had caught my gown on a nail in the door. I was watching you out of the corner of my eye. You were twirling your mustache, and you seemed quite vexed. You keep all the truffles for yourself—how nice of you! Not that one; I want that big black one there—in the corner. Well, after all, it was nonetheless very wrong, because—no, no, don't fill my glass; I don't want to get tipsy—because if we had not married (that might have happened, you know; they say that marriages hang by a thread), well, if the thread had not been strong enough, here I was left with that kiss on my shoulder—a pretty plight!"

"Nonsense! It does not stain."

"Yes, sir, it does; I beg your pardon, but it does stain, and so much so that there are husbands, I am told, who spill their blood to wash out those little stains."

"I was only jesting, dear. Heavens! I should think it did! Fancy! Why—"

"Ah, I am glad to hear you say so. I like to see you get angry. You are just a wee bit jealous, tell me, are you not? Well, upon my word! I asked you for the big black one, and you are quietly eating it!"

"I am very sorry, my love; I beg your pardon. I forgot all about it."

"Yes, just as you did when we were being married. I was obliged to touch your elbow to make you answer yes to Monsieur the Mayor's kind words!"

"Kind words?"

"Yes, kind words. I thought the Mayor was charming. No one could have been more happy than he was in addressing me. 'Mademoiselle, do you consent to take this great big ugly little man who stands beside you for your lawful—' [Laughing with her mouth full.] I was about to say to him, 'Let us understand each other, Monsieur; there is much to be said for and against.' Heavens! I am choking! [Bursts into great peals of laughter.] I was wrong in not making some restrictions. There! I am teasing you, and that is stupid. I said yes with my whole heart, I assure you, my darling, and the word was only too weak. When I think that all women, even the bad ones, use that same word, I feel ashamed of not having invented a better one. [Holding up her glass.] Here is to our golden wedding!"

"And here is to his christening, little mother!"

In an undertone: "Tell me, dear, are you sorry you married me?"

(Laughing.) "Yes. [Kissing her on the shoulder.] I think I have found the stain. Here it is."

"Do you realize that it is two o'clock. The fire is out. I am —you won't laugh? Well, I am just a little dizzy!"

"That was a famous *pâté!*"

"A famous *pâté!* We will have a cup of tea in the morning, eh, dear?"

Christmas Carol

by SARA TEASDALE

The kings they came from out the south,
   All dressed in ermine fine;
They bore Him gold and chrysoprase,
   And gifts of precious wine.

The shepherds came from out the north,
   Their coats were brown and old;
They brought Him little new-born lambs—
   They had not any gold.

The wise men came from out the east,
   And they were wrapped in white;
The star that led them all the way
   Did glorify the night.

The angels came from heaven high,
   And they were clad with wings;
And lo, they brought a joyful song
   The host of heaven sings.

The kings they knocked upon the door,
   The wise men entered in,
The shepherds followed after them
   To hear the song begin.

The angels sang through all the night
  Until the rising sun,
But little Jesus fell asleep
  Before the song was done.

The Adventure of
the Blue Carbuncle

(from *The Complete Sherlock Holmes*)

by ARTHUR CONAN DOYLE

I HAD called upon my friend Sherlock Holmes upon the second morning after Christmas, with the intention of wishing him the compliments of the season. He was lounging upon the sofa in a purple dressing-gown, a pipe-rack within his reach upon the right, and a pile of crumpled morning papers, evidently newly studied, near at hand. Beside the couch was a wooden chair, and on the angle of the back hung a very seedy and disreputable hard-felt hat, much the worse for wear, and cracked in several places. A lens and a forceps lying upon the seat of the chair suggested that the hat had been suspended in this manner for the purpose of examination.

"You are engaged," said I; "perhaps I interrupt you."

"Not at all. I am glad to have a friend with whom I can discuss my results. The matter is a perfectly trivial one"—he jerked his thumb in the direction of the old hat—"but there are points in connection with it which are not entirely devoid of interest and even of instruction."

I seated myself in his armchair and warmed my hands before his crackling fire, for a sharp frost had set in, and the windows were thick with the ice crystals. "I suppose," I remarked, "that, homely as it looks, this thing has some deadly story linked on to it—that it is the clue which will guide you in the solution of some mystery and the punishment of some crime."

"No, no. No crime," said Sherlock Holmes, laughing. "Only one of those whimsical little incidents which will happen when you have four million human beings all jostling each other within the space of a few square miles. Amid the action and reaction of so dense a swarm of humanity, every possible combination of events may be expected to take place, and many a little problem will be presented which may be striking and bizarre without being criminal. We have already had experience of such."

"So much so," I remarked, "that of the last six cases which I have added to my notes, three have been entirely free of any legal crime."

"Precisely. You allude to my attempt to recover the Irene Adler papers, to the singular case of Miss Mary Sutherland, and to the adventure of the man with the twisted lip. Well, I have no doubt that this small matter will fall into the same innocent category. You know Peterson, the commissionaire?"

"Yes."

"It is to him that this trophy belongs."

"It is his hat."

"No, no; he found it. Its owner is unknown. I beg that you will look upon it not as a battered billycock but as an intellectual problem. And, first, as to how it came here. It arrived upon Christmas morning, in company with a good fat goose, which is, I have no doubt, roasting at this moment in front of Peterson's fire. The facts are these: about four o'clock on Christmas morning, Peterson, who, as you know, is a very honest fellow, was returning from some small jollification and was making his way homeward down Tottenham Court Road. In front of him he saw, in the gaslight, a tallish man, walking with a slight stagger, and carrying a white goose slung over his shoulder. As he reached the corner of Goodge Street, a row broke out between this stranger and a little knot of roughs. One of the latter knocked off the man's hat, on which he raised his stick to defend himself and, swinging it over his head, smashed the shop window behind him. Peterson had rushed forward to protect the stranger from his assailants; but the man, shocked at having broken the window, and seeing an official-looking person in uniform rushing towards him, dropped his goose, took to his heels, and vanished amid the labyrinth of small streets which lie at the back of Tottenham Court Road. The roughs had also fled at the appearance of Peterson, so that he was left in possession of the field of battle, and also of the spoils of victory in the shape of this battered hat and a most unimpeachable Christmas goose."

"Which surely he restored to their owner?"

"My dear fellow, there lies the problem. It is true that 'For Mrs. Henry Baker' was printed upon a small card which was tied to the bird's left leg, and it is also true that the initials 'H. B.' are legible upon the lining of this hat; but as there are some thousands of Bakers, and some hundreds of Henry Bakers in this city of ours, it is not easy to restore lost property to any one of them."

"What, then, did Peterson do?"

"He brought round both hat and goose to me on Christmas morning, knowing that even the smallest problems are of interest to me. The goose we retained until this morning, when there were signs that, in spite of the slight frost, it would be well that it should be eaten without unnecessary delay. Its finder has carried it off, therefore, to fulfil the ultimate destiny of a goose, while I continue to retain the hat of the unknown gentleman who lost his Christmas dinner."

"Did he not advertise?"

"No."

"Then, what clue could you have as to his identity?"

"Only as much as we can deduce."

"From his hat?"

"Precisely."

"But you are joking. What can you gather from this old battered felt?"

"Here is my lens. You know my methods. What can you gather yourself as to the individuality of the man who has worn this article?"

I took the tattered object in my hands and turned it over rather ruefully. It was a very ordinary black hat of the usual round shape, hard and much the worse for wear. The lining had been of red silk, but was a good deal discoloured. There was no maker's name; but, as Holmes had remarked, the initials "H. B." were scrawled upon one side. It was pierced in the brim for a hat-securer, but the elastic was missing. For the rest, it was cracked, exceedingly dusty, and spotted in several places, although there seemed to have been some attempt to hide the discoloured patches by smearing them with ink.

"I can see nothing," said I, handing it back to my friend.

"On the contrary, Watson, you can see everything. You fail, however, to reason from what you see. You are too timid in drawing your inferences."

"Then, pray tell me what it is that you can infer from this hat?"

He picked it up and gazed at it in the peculiar introspective fashion which was characteristic of him. "It is perhaps less suggestive than it might have been," he remarked, "and yet there are a few inferences which are very distinct, and a few others which represent at least a strong balance of probability. That the man was highly intellectual is of course obvious upon the face of it, and also that he was fairly well-to-do within the last three years, although he has now fallen upon evil days. He had foresight, but has less now than formerly, pointing to a moral retrogression, which, when taken with the decline of his fortunes, seems to indicate some evil influence, probably drink, at work upon him. This may account also for the obvious fact that his wife has ceased to love him."

"My dear Holmes!"

"He has, however, retained some degree of self-respect," he continued, disregarding my remonstrance. "He is a man who leads a sedentary life, goes out little, is out of training entirely, is middle-aged, has grizzled hair which he has had cut within the last few days, and which he anoints with lime-cream. These are the more patent facts which are to be deduced from his hat. Also, by the way, that it is extremely improbable that he has gas laid on in his house."

"You are certainly joking, Holmes."

"Not in the least. Is it possible that even now, when I give you these results, you are unable to see how they are attained?"

"I have no doubt that I am very stupid, but I must confess that I am unable to follow you. For example, how did you deduce that this man was intellectual?"

For answer Holmes clapped the hat upon his head. It came right over the forehead and settled upon the bridge of his nose. "It is a question of cubic capacity," said he; "a man with so large a brain must have something in it."

"The decline of his fortunes, then?"

"This hat is three years old. These flat brims curled at the edge came in then. It is a hat of the very best quality. Look at the band of ribbed silk and the excellent lining. If this man could afford to buy so expensive a hat three years ago, and has had no hat since, then he has assuredly gone down in the world."

"Well, that is clear enough, certainly. But how about the foresight and the moral retrogression?"

Sherlock Holmes laughed. "Here is the foresight," said he, putting his finger upon the little disc and loop of the hat-securer. "They are never sold upon hats. If this man ordered one, it is a sign of a certain amount of foresight, since he went out of his way to take this precaution against the wind. But since we see that he has broken the elastic and has not troubled to replace it, it is obvious that he has less foresight now than formerly, which is a distinct proof of a weakening nature. On the other hand, he has endeavoured to conceal some of these stains upon the felt by daubing them with ink, which is a sign that he has not entirely lost his self-respect."

"Your reasoning is certainly plausible."

"The further points, that he is middle-aged, that his hair is grizzled, that it has been recently cut, and that he uses lime-cream, are all to be gathered from a close examination of the lower part of the lining. The lens discloses a large number of hair-ends, clean cut by the scissors of the barber. They all appear to be adhesive, and there is a distinct odour of lime-cream. This dust, you will observe, is not the gritty, gray dust of the street but the fluffy brown dust of the house, showing that it has been hung up indoors most of the time; while the marks of moisture upon the inside are proof positive that the wearer perspired very freely, and could, therefore, hardly be in the best of training."

"But his wife—you said that she had ceased to love him."

"This hat has not been brushed for weeks. When I see you, my dear Watson, with a week's accumulation of dust upon your hat, and when your wife allows you to go out in such a state, I shall fear that you also have been unfortunate enough to lose your wife's affection."

"But he might be a bachelor."

"Nay, he was bringing home the goose as a peace-offering to his wife. Remember the card upon the bird's leg."

"You have an answer to everything. But how on earth do you deduce that the gas is not laid on in his house?"

"One tallow stain, or even two, might come by chance; but when I see no less than five, I think that there can be little doubt that the individual must be brought into frequent contact with burning tallow—walks upstairs at night probably with his hat in one hand and a guttering candle in the other. Anyhow, he never got tallow-stains from a gas-jet. Are you satisfied?"

"Well, it is very ingenious," said I, laughing; "but since, as you said just now, there has been no crime committed, and no harm done save the loss of a goose, all this seems to be rather a waste of energy."

Sherlock Holmes had opened his mouth to reply, when the door flew open, and Peterson, the commissionaire, rushed into the apartment with flushed cheeks and the face of a man who is dazed with astonishment.

"The goose, Mr. Holmes! The goose, sir!" he gasped.

"Eh? What of it, then? Has it returned to life and flapped off through the kitchen window?" Holmes twisted himself round upon the sofa to get a fairer view of the man's excited face.

"See here, sir! See what my wife found in its crop!" He held out his hand and displayed upon the centre of the palm a brilliantly scintillating blue stone, rather smaller than a bean in size, but of such purity and radiance that it twinkled like an electric point in the dark hollow of his hand.

Sherlock Holmes sat up with a whistle. "By Jove, Peterson!" said he, "this is treasure trove indeed. I suppose you know what you have got?"

"A diamond, sir? A precious stone. It cuts into glass as though it were putty."

"It's more than a precious stone. It is *the* precious stone."

"Not the Countess of Morcar's blue carbuncle!" I ejaculated.

"Precisely so. I ought to know its size and shape, seeing that I have read the advertisement about it in *The Times* every day lately. It is absolutely unique, and its value can only be conjectured, but the reward offered of £1000 is certainly not within a twentieth part of the market price."

"A thousand pounds! Great Lord of mercy!" The commissionaire plumped down into a chair and stared from one to the other of us.

"That is the reward, and I have reason to know that there

are sentimental considerations in the background which would induce the Countess to part with half her fortune if she could but recover the gem."

"It was lost, if I remember aright, at the Hotel Cosmopolitan," I remarked.

"Precisely so, on December 22d, just five days ago. John Horner, a plumber, was accused of having abstracted it from the lady's jewel-case. The evidence against him was so strong that the case has been referred to the Assizes. I have some account of the matter here, I believe." He rummaged amid his newspapers, glancing over the dates, until at last he smoothed one out, doubled it over, and read the following paragraph:

"Hotel Cosmopolitan Jewel Robbery. John Horner, 26, plumber, was brought up upon the charge of having upon the 22nd inst., abstracted from the jewel-case of the Countess of Morcar the valuable gem known as the blue carbuncle. James Ryder, upper-attendant at the hotel, gave his evidence to the effect that he had shown Horner up to the dressing-room of the Countess of Morcar upon the day of the robbery in order that he might solder the second bar of the grate, which was loose. He had remained with Horner some little time, but had finally been called away. On returning, he found that Horner had disappeared, that the bureau had been forced open, and that the small morocco casket in which, as it afterwards transpired, the Countess was accustomed to keep her jewel, was lying empty upon the dressing-table. Ryder instantly gave the alarm, and Horner was arrested the same evening; but the stone could not be found either upon his person or in his rooms. Catherine Cusack, maid to the Countess, deposed to having heard Ryder's cry of dismay on discovering the robbery, and to having rushed into the room, where she found matters as described by the last witness. Inspector Bradstreet, B division, gave evidence as to the arrest of Horner, who struggled frantically, and protested his innocence in the strongest terms. Evidence of a previous conviction for robbery having been given against the prisoner, the magistrate refused to deal summarily with the offence, but referred it to the Assizes. Horner, who had shown signs of intense emotion during the proceedings, fainted away at the conclusion and was carried out of court.

"Hum! So much for the police-court," said Holmes thoughtfully, tossing aside the paper. "The question for us now to solve is the sequence of events leading from a rifled jewel-case at one end to the crop of a goose in Tottenham Court Road at the other. You see, Watson, our little deductions have suddenly assumed a much more important and less innocent aspect. Here is the stone; the stone came from the goose, and the goose came from Mr. Henry Baker, the gentleman with the bad hat and all the other characteristics with which I have bored you. So now we must set ourselves very seriously to finding this gentleman and ascertaining what part he has played in this little mystery. To do this, we must try the simplest means first, and these lie undoubtedly in an advertisement in all the evening papers. If this fail, I shall have recourse to other methods."

"What will you say?"

"Give me a pencil and that slip of paper. Now, then:

"Found at the corner of Goodge Street, a goose and a black felt hat. Mr. Henry Baker can have the same by applying at 6:30 this evening at 221B, Baker Street.

That is clear and concise."

"Very. But will he see it?"

"Well, he is sure to keep an eye on the papers, since, to a poor man, the loss was a heavy one. He was clearly so scared by his mischance in breaking the window and by the approach of Peterson that he thought of nothing but flight, but since then he must have bitterly regretted the impulse which caused him to drop his bird. Then, again, the introduction of his name will cause him to see it, for everyone who knows him will direct his attention to it. Here you are, Peterson, run down to the advertising agency and have this put in the evening papers."

"In which, sir?"

"Oh, in the *Globe, Star, Pall Mall, St. James's, Evening News Standard, Echo,* and any others that occur to you."

"Very well, sir. And this stone?"

"Ah, yes, I shall keep the stone. Thank you. And, I say, Peterson, just buy a goose on your way back and leave it here with me, for we must have one to give to this gentleman in place of the one which your family is now devouring."

When the commissionaire had gone, Holmes took up the stone and held it against the light. "It's a bonny thing," said he. "Just see how it glints and sparkles. Of course it is a nucleus and focus of crime. Every good stone is. They are the devil's pet baits. In the larger and older jewels every facet may stand for a bloody deed. This stone is not yet twenty years old. It was found in the banks of the Amoy River in southern China and is remarkable in having every characteristic of the carbuncle, save that it is blue in shade instead of ruby red. In spite of its youth, it has already a sinister history. There have been two murders, a vitriol-throwing, a suicide, and several robberies brought about for the sake of this forty-grain weight of crystallized charcoal. Who would think that so pretty a toy would be a purveyor to the gallows and the prison? I'll lock it up in my strong box now and drop a line to the Countess to say that we have it."

"Do you think that this man Horner is innocent?"

"I cannot tell."

"Well, then, do you imagine that this other one, Henry Baker, had anything to do with the matter?"

"It is, I think, much more likely that Henry Baker is an absolutely innocent man, who had no idea that the bird which he was carrying was of considerably more value than if it were made of solid gold. That, however, I shall determine by a very simple test if we have an answer to our advertisement."

"And you can do nothing until then?"

"Nothing."

"In that case I shall continue my professional round. But I shall come back in the evening at the hour you have mentioned, for I should like to see the solution of so tangled a business."

"Very glad to see you. I dine at seven. There is a woodcock, I believe. By the way, in view of recent occurrences, perhaps I ought to ask Mrs. Hudson to examine its crop."

I had been delayed at a case, and it was a little after half-past six when I found myself in Baker Street once more. As I approached the house I saw a tall man in a Scotch bonnet with a coat which was buttoned up to his chin waiting outside in the bright semicircle which was thrown from the fanlight. Just as I arrived the door was opened, and we were shown up together to Holmes's room.

"Mr. Henry Baker, I believe," said he, rising from his armchair and greeting his visitor with the easy air of geniality which he could so readily assume. "Pray take this chair by the fire, Mr. Baker. It is a cold night, and I observe that your circulation is more adapted for summer than for winter. Ah, Watson, you have just come at the right time. Is that your hat, Mr. Baker?"

"Yes, sir, that is undoubtedly my hat."

He was a large man with rounded shoulders, a massive head, and a broad, intelligent face, sloping down to a pointed beard of grizzled brown. A touch of red in nose and cheeks, with a slight tremor of his extended hand, recalled Holmes's surmise as to his habits. His rusty black frock-coat was buttoned right up in front, with the collar turned up, and his lank wrists protruded from his sleeves without a sign of cuff or shirt. He spoke in a slow staccato fashion, choosing his words with care, and gave the impression generally of a man of learning and letters who had had ill-usage at the hands of fortune.

"We have retained these things for some days," said Holmes, "because we expected to see an advertisement from you giving your address. I am at a loss to know now why you did not advertise."

Our visitor gave a rather shamefaced laugh. "Shillings have not been so plentiful with me as they once were," he remarked. "I had no doubt that the gang of roughs who assaulted me had carried off both my hat and the bird. I did not care to spend more money in a hopeless attempt at recovering them."

"Very naturally. By the way, about the bird, we were compelled to eat it."

"To eat it!" Our visitor half rose from his chair in his excitement.

"Yes, it would have been of no use to anyone had we not done so. But I presume that this other goose upon the sideboard, which is about the same weight and perfectly fresh, will answer your purpose equally well?"

"Oh, certainly, certainly," answered Mr. Baker with a sigh of relief.

"Of course, we still have the feathers, legs, crop, and so on of your own bird, so if you wish——"

The man burst into a hearty laugh. "They might be useful to me as relics of my adventure," said he, "but beyond that I can hardly see what use the *disjecta membra* of my late acquaintance are going to be to me. No, sir, I think that, with your permission, I will confine my attentions to the excellent bird which I perceive upon the sideboard."

Sherlock Holmes glanced sharply across at me with a slight shrug of his shoulders.

"There is your hat, then, and there your bird," said he. "By the way, would it bore you to tell me where you got the other one from? I am somewhat of a fowl fancier, and I have seldom seen a better grown goose."

"Certainly, sir," said Baker, who had risen and tucked his newly gained property under his arm. "There are a few of us who frequent the Alpha Inn, near the Museum—we are to be found in the Museum itself during the day, you understand. This year our good host, Windigate by name, instituted a goose club, by which, on consideration of some few pence every week, we were each to receive a bird at Christmas. My pence were duly paid, and the rest is familiar to you. I am much indebted to you, sir, for a Scotch bonnet is fitted neither to my years nor my gravity." With a comical pomposity of manner he bowed solemnly to both of us and strode off upon his way.

"So much for Mr. Henry Baker," said Holmes when he had closed the door behind him. "It is quite certain that he knows nothing whatever about the matter. Are you hungry, Watson?"

"Not particularly."

"Then I suggest that we turn our dinner into a supper and follow up this clue while it is still hot."

"By all means."

It was a bitter night, so we drew on our ulsters and wrapped cravats about our throats. Outside, the stars were shining coldly in a cloudless sky, and the breath of the passers-by blew out into smoke like so many pistol shots. Our footfalls rang out crisply and loudly as we swung through the doctors' quarter, Wimpole Street, Harley Street, and so through Wigmore Street into Oxford Street. In a quarter of an hour we were in Bloomsbury at the Alpha Inn, which is a small public-house at the corner of one of the streets which runs down into Holborn. Holmes pushed open the door of the private bar and ordered two glasses of beer from the ruddy-faced, white-aproned landlord.

"Your beer should be excellent if it is as good as your geese," said he.

"My geese!" The man seemed surprised.

"Yes. I was speaking only half an hour ago to Mr. Henry Baker, who was a member of your goose club."

"Ah! yes, I see. But you see, sir, them's not *our* geese."

"Indeed! Whose, then?"

"Well, I got the two dozen from a salesman in Covent Garden."

"Indeed? I know some of them. Which was it?"

"Breckinridge is his name."

"Ah! I don't know him. Well, here's your good health, landlord, and prosperity to your house. Good-night.

"Now for Mr. Breckinridge," he continued, buttoning up his coat as we came out into the frosty air. "Remember, Watson, that though we have so homely a thing as a goose at one end of this chain, we have at the other a man who will certainly get seven years' penal servitude unless we can establish his innocence. It is possible that our inquiry may but confirm his guilt; but, in any case, we have a line of investigation which has been missed by the police, and which a singular chance has placed in our hands. Let us follow it out to the bitter end. Faces to the south, then, and quick march!"

We passed across Holborn, down Endell Street, and so through a zigzag of slums to Covent Garden Market. One of the largest stalls bore the name of Breckinridge upon it, and the proprietor, a horsy-looking man, with a sharp face and trim side-whiskers, was helping a boy to put up the shutters.

"Good-evening. It's a cold night," said Holmes.

The salesman nodded and shot a questioning glance at my companion.

"Sold out of geese, I see," continued Holmes, pointing at the bare slabs of marble.

"Let you have five hundred to-morrow morning."

"That's no good."

"Well, there are some on the stall with the gas-flare."

"Ah, but I was recommended to you."

"Who by?"

"The landlord of the Alpha."

"Oh, yes; I sent him a couple of dozen."

"Fine birds they were, too. Now where did you get them from?"

To my surprise the question provoked a burst of anger from the salesman.

"Now, then, mister," said he, with his head cocked and his arms akimbo, "what are you driving at? Let's have it straight, now."

"It is straight enough. I should like to know who sold you the geese which you supplied to the Alpha."

"Well, then, I shan't tell you. So now!"

"Oh, it is a matter of no importance; but I don't know why you should be so warm over such a trifle."

"Warm! You'd be as warm, maybe, if you were as pestered as I am. When I pay good money for a good article there should be an end of the business; but it's 'Where are the geese?' and 'Who did you sell the geese to?' and 'What will you take for the geese?' One would think they were the only geese in the world, to hear the fuss that is made over them."

"Well, I have no connection with any other peole who have been making inquiries," said Holmes carelessly. "If you won't tell us the bet is off, that is all. But I'm always ready to back my opinion on a matter of fowls, and I have a fiver on it that the bird I ate is country bred."

"Well, then, you've lost your fiver, for it's town bred," snapped the salesman.

"It's nothing of the kind."

"I say it is."

"I don't believe it."

"D'you think you know more about fowls than I, who have

handled them ever since I was a nipper? I tell you, all those birds that went to the Alpha were town bred."

"You'll never persuade me to believe that."

"Will you bet, then?"

"It's merely taking your money, for I know that I am right. But I'll have a sovereign on with you, just to teach you not to be obstinate."

The salesman chuckled grimly. "Bring me the books, Bill," said he.

The small boy brought round a small thin volume and a great greasy-backed one, laying them out together beneath the hanging lamp.

"Now then, Mr. Cocksure," said the salesman, "I thought that I was out of geese, but before I finish you'll find that there is still one left in my shop. You see this little book?"

"Well?"

"That's the list of the folk from whom I buy. D'you see? Well, then, here on this page are the country folk, and the numbers after their names are where their accounts are in the big ledger. Now, then! You see this other page in red ink? Well, that is a list of my town suppliers. Now, look at that third name. Just read it out to me."

"Mrs. Oakshott, 117, Brixton Road—249," read Holmes.

"Quite so. Now turn that up in the ledger."

Holmes turned to the page indicated. "Here you are, 'Mrs. Oakshott, 117, Brixton Road, egg and poultry supplier.'"

"Now, then, what's the last entry?"

"'December 22d. Twenty-four geese at 7s. 6d.'"

"Quite so. There you are. And underneath?"

"'Sold to Mr. Windigate of the Alpha, at 12s.'"

"What have you to say now?"

Sherlock Holmes looked deeply chagrined. He drew a sovereign from his pocket and threw it down upon the slab, turning away with the air of a man whose disgust is too deep for words. A few yards off he stopped under a lamp-post and laughed in the hearty, noiseless fashion which was peculiar to him.

"When you see a man with whiskers of that cut and the 'Pink 'un' protruding out of his pocket, you can always draw him by a bet," said he. "I daresay that if I had put £100 down in front of him, that man would not have given me such complete information as was drawn from him by the idea that he was doing me on a wager. Well, Watson, we are, I fancy, nearing the end of our quest, and the only point which remains to be determined is whether we should go on to this Mrs. Oakshott to-night, or whether we should reserve it for to-morrow. It is clear from what that surly fellow said that there are others besides ourselves who are anxious about the matter, and I should——"

His remarks were suddenly cut short by a loud hubbub which broke out from the stall which we had just left. Turning round we saw a little rat-faced fellow standing in the centre of the circle of yellow light which was thrown by the swinging lamp, while Breckinridge, the salesman, framed in the door of his stall, was shaking his fists fiercely at the cringing figure.

"I've had enough of you and your geese," he shouted. "I wish you were all at the devil together. If you come pestering me any more with your silly talk I'll set the dog at you. You bring Mrs. Oakshott here and I'll answer her, but what have you to do with it? Did I buy the geese off you?"

"No; but one of them was mine all the same," whined the little man.

"Well, then, ask Mrs. Oakshott for it."

"She told me to ask you."

"Well, you can ask the King of Proosia, for all I care. I've had enough of it. Get out of this!" He rushed fiercely forward, and the inquirer flitted away into the darkness.

"Ha! this may save us a visit to Brixton Road," whispered Holmes. "Come with me, and we will see what is to be made of this fellow." Striding through the scattered knots of people who lounged round the flaring stalls, my companion speedily overtook the little man and touched him upon the shoulder. He sprang round, and I could see in the gas-light that every vestige of colour had been driven from his face.

"Who are you, then? What do you want?" he asked in a quavering voice.

"You will excuse me," said Holmes blandly, "but I could not help overhearing the questions which you put to the salesman just now. I think that I could be of assistance to you."

"You? Who are you? How could you know anything of the matter?"

"My name is Sherlock Holmes. It is my business to know what other people don't know."

"But you can know nothing of this?"

"Excuse me, I know everything of it. You are endeavouring to trace some geese which were sold by Mrs. Oakshott, of Brixton Road, to a salesman named Breckinridge, by him in turn to Mr. Windigate, of the Alpha, and by him to his club, of which Mr. Henry Baker is a member."

"Oh, sir, you are the very man whom I have longed to meet," cried the little fellow with outstretched hands and quivering fingers. "I can hardly explain to you how interested I am in this matter."

Sherlock Holmes hailed a four-wheeler which was passing. "In that case we had better discuss it in a cosy room rather than in this wind-swept market-place," said he. "But pray tell me, before we go farther, who it is that I have the pleasure of assisting."

The man hesitated for an instant. "My name is John Robinson," he answered with a sidelong glance.

"No, no; the real name," said Holmes sweetly. "It is always awkward doing business with an alias."

A flush sprang to the white cheeks of the stranger. "Well, then," said he, "my real name is James Ryder."

"Precisely so. Head attendant at the Hotel Cosmopolitan. Pray step into the cab, and I shall soon be able to tell you everything which you would wish to know."

The little man stood glancing from one to the other of us with half-frightened, half-hopeful eyes, as one who is not sure whether he is on the verge of a windfall or of a catastrophe. Then he stepped into the cab, and in half an hour we were back in the sitting-room at Baker Street. Nothing had been said during our drive, but the high, thin breathing of our new companion, and the claspings and unclaspings of his hands, spoke of the nervous tension within him.

"Here we are!" said Holmes cheerily as we filed into the room. "The fire looks very seasonable in this weather. You look cold, Mr. Ryder. Pray take the basket-chair. I will just put on my slippers before we settle this little matter of yours. Now, then! You want to know what became of those geese?"

"Yes, sir."

"Or rather, I fancy, of that goose. It was one bird, I imagine, in which you were interested—white, with a black bar across the tail."

Ryder quivered with emotion. "Oh, sir," he cried, "can you tell me where it went to?"

"It came here."

"Here?"

"Yes, and a most remarkable bird it proved. I don't wonder that you should take an interest in it. It laid an egg after it was dead—the bonniest, brightest little blue egg that ever was seen. I have it here in my museum."

Our visitor staggered to his feet and clutched the mantel-piece with his right hand. Holmes unlocked his strong-box and held up the blue carbuncle, which shone out like a star, with a cold, brilliant, many-pointed radiance. Ryder stood glaring with a drawn face, uncertain whether to claim or to disown it.

"The game's up, Ryder," said Holmes quietly. "Hold up,

man, or you'll be into the fire! Give him an arm back into his chair, Watson. He's not got blood enough to go in for felony with impunity. Give him a dash of brandy. So! Now he looks a little more human. What a shrimp it is, to be sure!"

For a moment he had staggered and nearly fallen, but the brandy brought a tinge of colour into his cheeks, and he sat staring with frightened eyes at his accuser.

"I have almost every link in my hands, and all the proofs which I could possibly need, so there is little which you need tell me. Still, that little may as well be cleared up to make the case complete. You had heard, Ryder, of this blue stone of the Countess of Morcar's?"

"It was Catherine Cusack who told me of it," said he in a crackling voice.

"I see—her ladyship's waiting-maid. Well, the temptation of sudden wealth so easily acquired was too much for you, as it has been for better men before you; but you were not very scrupulous in the means you used. It seems to me, Ryder, that there is the making of a very pretty villain in you. You knew that this man Horner, the plumber, had been concerned in some such matter before, and that suspicion would rest the more readily upon him. What did you do, then? You made some small job in my lady's room—you and your confederate Cusack—and you managed that he should be the man sent for. Then, when he had left, you rifled the jewel-case, raised the alarm, and had this unfortunate man arrested. You then——"

Ryder threw himself down suddenly upon the rug and clutched at my companion's knees. "For God's sake, have mercy!" he shrieked. "Think of my father! of my mother! It would break their hearts. I never went wrong before! I never will again. I swear it. I'll swear it on a Bible. Oh, don't bring it into court! For Christ's sake, don't!"

"Get back into your chair!" said Holmes sternly. "It is very well to cringe and crawl now, but you thought little enough of this poor Horner in the dock for a crime of which he knew nothing."

"I will fly, Mr. Holmes. I will leave the country, sir. Then the charge against him will break down."

"Hum! We will talk about that. And now let us hear a true account of the next act. How came the stone into the goose, and how came the goose into the open market? Tell us the truth, for there lies your only hope of safety."

Ryder passed his tongue over his parched lips. "I will tell you it just as it happened, sir," said he. "When Horner had been arrested, it seemed to me that it would be best for me to get away with the stone at once, for I did not know at what moment the police might not take it into their heads to search me and my room. There was no place about the hotel where it would be safe. I went out, as if on some commission, and I made for my sister's house. She had married a man named Oakshott, and lived in Brixton Road, where she fattened fowls for the market. All the way there every man I met seemed to me to be a policeman or a detective; and, for all that it was a cold night, the sweat was pouring down my face before I came to the Brixton Road. My sister asked me what was the matter, and why I was so pale; but I told her that I had been upset by the jewel robbery at the hotel. Then I went into the back yard and smoked a pipe, and wondered what it would be best to do.

"I had a friend once called Maudsley, who went to the bad, and has just been serving his time in Pentonville. One day he had met me, and fell into talk about the ways of thieves, and how they could get rid of what they stole. I knew that he would be true to me, for I knew one or two things about him; so I made up my mind to go right on to Kilburn, where he lived, and take him into my confidence. He would show me how to turn the stone into money. But how to get to him in safety? I thought of the agonies I had gone through in coming from the hotel. I might at any moment be seized and searched, and there would be the stone in my waistcoat pocket. I was leaning against the wall at the time and looking at the geese which were waddling about round my feet, and suddenly an idea came into my head which showed me how I could beat the best detective that ever lived.

"My sister had told me some weeks before that I might have the pick of her geese for a Christmas present, and I knew that she was always as good as her word. I would take my goose now, and in it I would carry my stone to Kilburn. There was a little shed in the yard, and behind this I drove one of the birds—a fine big one, white, with a barred tail. I caught it, and, prying its bill open, I thrust the stone down its throat as far as my finger could reach. The bird gave a gulp, and I felt the stone pass along its gullet and down into its crop. But the creature flapped and struggled, and out came my sister to know what was the matter. As I turned to speak to her the brute broke loose and fluttered off among the others.

" 'Whatever were you doing with that bird, Jem?' says she.

" 'Well,' said I, 'you said you'd give me one for Christmas, and I was feeling which was the fattest.'

" 'Oh,' says she, 'we've set yours aside for you—Jem's bird, we call it. It's the big white one over yonder. There's twenty-six of them, which makes one for you, and one for us, and two dozen for the market.'

" 'Thank you, Maggie,' says I; 'but if it is all the same to you, I'd rather have that one I was handling just now.'

" 'The other is a good three pound heavier,' said she, 'and we fattened it expressly for you.'

" 'Never mind. I'll have the other, and I'll take it now,' said I.

" 'Oh, just as you like,' said she, a little huffed. 'Which is it you want, then?'

" 'That white one with the barred tail, right in the middle of the flock.'

" 'Oh, very well. Kill it and take it with you.'

"Well, I did what she said, Mr. Holmes, and I carried the bird all the way to Kilburn. I told my pal what I had done, for he was a man that it was easy to tell a thing like that to. He laughed until he choked, and we got a knife and opened the goose. My heart turned to water, for there was no sign of the stone, and I knew that some terrible mistake had occurred. I left the bird, rushed back to my sister's, and hurried into the back yard. There was not a bird to be seen there.

" 'Where are they all, Maggie?' I cried.

" 'Gone to the dealer's, Jem.'

" 'Which dealer's?'

" 'Breckinridge, of Covent Garden.'

" 'But was there another with a barred tail?' I asked, 'the same as the one I chose?'

" 'Yes, Jem; there were two barred-tailed ones, and I could never tell them apart.'

"Well, then, of course I saw it all, and I ran off as hard as my feet would carry me to this man Breckinridge; but he had sold the lot at once, and not one word would he tell me as to where they had gone. You heard him yourselves to-night. Well, he has always answered me like that. My sister thinks that I am going mad. Sometimes I think that I am myself. And now—and now I am myself a branded thief, without ever having touched the wealth for which I sold my character. God help me! God help me!" He burst into convulsive sobbing, with his face buried in his hands.

There was a long silence, broken only by his heavy breathing, and by the measured tapping of Sherlock Holmes's finger-tips upon the edge of the table. Then my friend rose and threw open the door.

"Get out!" said he.

"What, sir! Oh, Heaven bless you!"

"No more words. Get out!"

And no more words were needed. There was a rush, a clatter upon the stairs, the bang of a door, and the crisp rattle of running footfalls from the street.

"After all, Watson," said Holmes, reaching up his hand for his clay pipe, "I am not retained by the police to supply their deficiencies. If Horner were in danger it would be another thing; but this fellow will not appear against him, and the case must collapse. I suppose that I am commuting a felony, but it is just possible that I am saving a soul. This fellow will not go wrong again; he is too terribly frightened. Send him to jail now, and you make him a jail-bird for life. Besides, it is the season of forgiveness. Chance has put in our way a most singular and whimsical problem, and its solution is its own reward. If you will have the goodness to touch the bell, Doctor, we will begin another investigation, in which, also, a bird will be the chief feature."

The Three Ships

by ALFRED NOYES

As I went up the mountain-side
The sea below me glitter'd wide,
And, Eastward, far away, I spied
 On Christmas Day, on Christmas Day,
The three great ships that take the tide
 On Christmas Day in the morning.

Ye have heard the song, how these must ply
From the harbours of home to the ports o' the sky!
Do ye dream none knoweth the whither and why
 On Christmas Day, on Christmas Day
The three great ships go sailing by
 On Christmas Day in the morning?

Yet, as I live, I never knew
That ever a song could ring so true,
Till I saw them break thro' a haze of blue
 On Christmas Day, on Christmas Day;
And the marvellous ancient flags they flew
 On Christmas Day in the morning!

From the heights above the belfried town
I saw that the sails were patched and brown,
But the flags were a-flame with a great renown
 On Christmas Day, on Christmas Day,
And on every mast was a golden crown
 On Christmas Day in the morning.

The Three Ships

Most marvellous ancient ships were these!
Were their prows a-plunge to the Chersonese,
For the pomp of Rome, or the glory of Greece,
    On Christmas Day, on Christmas Day?
Were they out on a quest for the Golden Fleece
    On Christmas Day in the morning?

The sun and the wind they told me there
How goodly a load the three ships bear,
For the first is gold and the second is myrrh
    On Christmas Day, on Christmas Day;
And the third is frankincense most rare,
    On Christmas Day in the morning.

They have mixed their shrouds with the golden sky,
They have faded away where the last dreams die . . .
Ah yet, will ye watch, when the mist lifts high
    On Christmas Day, on Christmas Day?
Will ye see three ships come sailing by
    On Christmas Day in the morning?